Love Stories in This Town

Amanda Eyre Ward

# Love Stories
## IN THIS TOWN

BALLANTINE BOOKS

*New York*

A Ballantine Books Trade Paperback Original

Copyright © 2009 by Amanda Eyre Ward
Reading group guide copyright © 2009 by Random House, Inc.

Published in the United States by Ballantine Books, an imprint of The Random House Publishing Group, a division of Random House, Inc., New York.

Stories from this collection have appeared, in slightly different form, in the following publications:
"Should I Be Scared?" in *Pindeldyboz;* "Butte as in Beautiful" in the *New Delta Review;* "The Stars Are Bright in Texas" in *Zoetrope: All Story;* "Shakespeare.com" in *StoryQuarterly;* "The Way the Sky Changed" in *Tin House* and *The Best of Tin House;* "Miss Montana's Wedding Day" in the *Austin Chronicle;* and "Motherhood and Terrorism" in *Politically Inspired.*

ISBN 978-0-8129-8011-0
eBook ISBN 978-0-3455-1491-2

Printed in the United States of America

www.randomhousereaderscircle.com

2 4 6 8 9 7 5 3 1

Book design by Casey Hampton

*For Barbara and Larry,*
*Mom and Peter,*
*Dad and Cassia,*
*Sarah and Chris,*
*Liza and Brad,*
*and my love, Tip*

# Contents

# PART ONE

# Should I Be Scared?

I first heard about Cipro at the potluck.

"Thank God I've got Cipro," said Zelda. "My doctor prescribed it for a urinary tract infection, and I still have half the pills."

"Cipro?" I said, my mouth full of artichoke dip.

"Honey," said Zelda, "where have you been?"

It was a cold, clear night in Austin, Texas. After the disgusting heat of summer, the cool was a balm. Zelda wore a giant sweater, knit loosely from rough, rusty-colored wool. She stood next to the barbecue, holding her hands in front of the hot coals. In the kitchen, my husband and his scientist friends concocted an elaborate marinade.

"Anthrax," whispered Zelda. She had just begun to date my husband's thesis advisor, and lent an air of glamour to departmental potlucks.

"Excuse me?" I said. I took a large sip of wine, which had come from a cardboard box.

"Ciprofloxacin," clarified Zelda, hissing over the syllables. "It's the anthrax vaccine. A super-antibiotic. If we're dropped on by, like, a crop duster, Cipro is what you'll need. And," she lowered her voice again, "there isn't enough for everyone."

Zelda wore scarves and held her wineglass with her hands wrapped around the bowl. When she sipped, her eyes peered over the top, bright coins. She wore high leather boots and worked in a steel building downtown for a company that made expensive software. She had described her job to me: "It's an output management solution, and I market it. It connects the world." We had no idea why Zelda wanted to spend her evenings, which could obviously be spent in snazzier locales, with us. We wore Birkenstocks.

I was a scientist's wife. This title pleased me. I also worked at Ceramic City, where people could paint their own pottery. My title at Ceramic City was "color consultant." This title did not please me. I was trying to figure out what to do with my Bachelor of Arts degree in Anthropology, with a focus on the egalitarian foragers of the Kalahari Desert.

"Oh," I said to Zelda, regarding the Cipro. It was times like this that I felt lucky to have a scientist for a husband. I could ask him later for details, and he would not laugh at me. He explained things patiently, drawing circles and arrows on the margins of the newspaper.

"Hey, ladies!" said a dark figure, emerging from the kitchen. It was my husband's thesis advisor. "Is that fire ready for some birds?"

Zelda smiled charmingly. The light from the coals made her look a little scary when she turned to me.

"Get some for yourself," she said in a quiet voice. "I'm serious," she said, and then she turned her face up to meet her lover's lips.

My husband explained in the dark of our bedroom that ingesting expensive antibiotics for no reason was a bad course of action. We had pulled the covers over our heads and invited the cat into the warm cave. My husband called the cat "spelunker," saying, "What do you think, little spelunker? Do you think we should let the terrorists make us afraid? Do you think we should buy canned goods and a six-day supply of water?" (The last was in reference to my actions of the previous day, when I had arrived home with twenty-eight cans of Progresso soup and three gallons of water.)

This was the beginning of the War on Terrorism.

Two weeks before, we had discussed what to eat for dinner and if we were drinking too much beer. We had talked about having a baby, mowing the lawn, and what sort of dog we should adopt. (My husband was partial to standard poodles, and I liked little dogs that could sit in your lap or in your purse. If you carried a purse.)

In those days—which seemed impossibly bright now, untarnished—we had talked idly about what sort of fishing rod my husband should buy with his jar of quarters. My husband came home each night, took the change from his pants pocket, and dropped it into a large water jug; he claimed he had done this since he was six years old, and the first time the jug filled (right before I met him), he bought a canoe. The canoe! He loved it ferociously. He named the canoe after me, wrote my name in Wite-Out on the side. One night, when I was reading and he was asleep, he spoke. "You're the best," he said, his arms around my waist, squeezing. I checked: he was in dreamland, speaking from that place. "You're the best," he repeated. "You're the best, best, best canoe in the world."

In the end, we had decided that we wanted a baby more than a dog or a fishing rod, and we had thrown away my birth control pills and made love slowly, with the moon shining a soft light over us.

Things had changed so quickly and forcefully that it seemed to me my husband hadn't quite accepted the fact that we were in danger. I lay in bed in the mornings now, hearing helicopters and listening to the news.

"Your dad is making fun of me," I told the cat under the covers. I began to cry a little, and my husband said he was sorry.

The next morning, from behind the counter at Ceramic City, I called Dr. Fern. The first time the nurse answered, I hung up. I was alone in Ceramic City, but I did not know what to say to the nurse. Was I being crazy? I wanted to think so. My mother, who lived in Connecticut and had gone to three funerals for her friends' sons, told me that it was unpatriotic to want some Cipro for myself. When I told her I was afraid to get out of bed, she said, "That's just how the terrorists want you to feel."

I called Dr. Fern again. This time, when the nurse answered, I said that I would like to make an appointment.

"Issue?" said the nurse.

"Excuse me?" I said. A man peeked into the window of Ceramic City. I thought, Fuck.

"What is the issue," said the nurse, "that you need to see the doctor about?"

"Uh, I'd like to get a prescription," I said.

"For?"

"For ciprofloxacin," I said. The peeking man came inside and began to wander around, inspecting Personalized Pottery.

"Beg pardon?" said the nurse. Was she instructed not to use full sentences?

"In case of an anthrax attack on America," I said, "I would like to have my own supply of antibiotics." The man was holding a blue bowl painted with fish. He stared at me.

"Oh my," said the nurse.

"Well, so," I said. I put my hand over the mouthpiece. "Can I be of assistance?" I asked the man.

"My wife's birthday is Tuesday," he said.

"One moment, please," I said. The nurse told me that she would have to consult with the doctor and get back to me. She took my number. When I hung up the phone, I saw that the man had put the bowl back on the shelf.

"Should I be scared?" he asked.

. . .

The nurse called later that afternoon and explained in no uncertain terms that the doctor would not give me the drugs I had requested. She added that it was against every tenet of the medical establishment to prescribe drugs when a patient was not ill. I hung up the phone, instead of saying, "You self-important bitch." At home that evening, I cried again.

My husband watched me skeptically. We were eating Freebird burritos, sitting on our front porch and peeling off aluminum foil in small, metal circles. "We're not going to get anthrax," said my husband. He made a sound that I would classify as an incredulous snort.

"I know!" I said. I bit into my burrito, which I had ordered with extra guacamole. Extras were a dollar, and usually I refrained, but I had the feeling that I should live life to the fullest, and make a celebration of every day.

"And I want you to stop watching so much television," said my husband. He had been talking, it seemed, for some time. I nodded, and he turned his head toward me, squinting as if I were a scientific mystery. "Oh, honey," he said.

Nonetheless, I did watch television that night after my husband had fallen asleep. I sat in the front room in my pajamas, watching bombs and food rations fall. I drank a warm glass of milk and watched dirty children rip open bags of Pop-Tarts and jam them into their mouths.

The next day, I discovered an advertisement for Cipro on the back page of the *Austin Chronicle*. There it was, sandwiched between a massage therapist and a Spanish tutor: CIPRO

AVAILABLE 1-800-CIPRONOW. (The last "W," it seemed, was for effect.) Ceramic City was empty again, and I picked up the phone.

When I got home that evening, my husband was making linguine with clams. There was an open bottle of wine on the table, and two wineglasses. My husband had gone to some trouble: cloth napkins, the whole nine yards. In the kitchen, he was stirring dinner and leafing through a fishing catalog. I came into the kitchen and put my arms around him. "I'm your apron," I said.

"Look at this," said my husband, pointing to the catalog. "A baby-size fishing rod. I can take our little boy out in the canoe."

"Or our little girl," I said.

"Whatever," said my husband. "Either way, the change jar is now officially for the baby. For a little fishing rod, or maybe a little life vest."

As we ate the linguine, which was delicious, I brought up the Cipro. I explained that the pills we needed to stay alive for ten days would cost three hundred dollars. My husband put down his napkin, and looked at the table. He unclenched his fists and placed each hand carefully on either side of his plate. Finally, he lifted his head. He took a breath, and I saw him make the decision to act rationally. "We don't have any money," he said.

"Well," I said, "we do have the change jar." My husband nodded, his eyes closed. "If we die of anthrax," I said, "what will a fishing vest be good for?" Even I could tell I sounded hysterical. We sat in silence and finished the bottle of wine.

My husband then stood up and left the room. He came back with the jar, which he overturned. Years of change spilled over the floor.

"It happened without them knowing," I said. "I want to be ready."

My husband did not look at me. He sat cross-legged on the floor and began counting. The change jar added up to one hundred seventy-two dollars and sixteen cents.

"What are we going to do?" I said.

"Just get half," said my husband. "Save yourself," he said. And then he went and took the sleeping bag from the closet, and he placed it on the couch.

"I'll get enough for both of us, for five days," I said. "Five days will be enough to figure something out." I stood next to the couch, where my husband was feigning sleep. "I'm just asking for five days," I said. "I don't think that's unreasonable."

The man at 1-800-CIPRONOW had told me to meet him in the alley between San Antonio and Sixth. I drove there the next morning, a plastic bag of change in the passenger seat. "You'll be glad," I told my husband. "You'll thank me later."

The CIPRONOW man was Hispanic. He wore tight Wrangler jeans and a T-shirt with an American flag. Over the phone, he had explained that the Cipro was his mother's prescription; she needed money more than the drugs.

The man, whose flag shirt, upon closer inspection, was not very clean, was unhappy about splitting up the prescription. "What you need," he said, "is the full thirty pills. Three times a day for ten days. That's what you need."

"I'm sorry," I said, gesturing to the bag. "This is all I have."

"All you have," said the man, and he laughed. I blinked. "No deal," said the man, shaking his head.

"Well, fuck," I said. The change bag and I drove away.

That evening, as my husband grilled hamburgers in the backyard, I thought about how to get another hundred dollars and change. With our student loans, there just wasn't a dime to spare. "I already gave you all my money," my husband said, dramatically. "You can't live your life this way," he said, among other comments that amounted to same.

"I can sell something," I said.

"Oh really?" said my husband. He put his hands on his hips, and the spatula stuck out awkwardly. "Really?" he said. "What do you have to sell?"

I did not answer. The damn fact was that I had nothing to sell. My books, maybe, or my bod. Unhappily, neither would likely bring a hundred dollars. I did not sleep that night. I lay awake, and dreamed about dying horribly, with lots of gasping. Worse, I dreamed of life without my husband, our house, our canoe. I dreamed of living in a cave, with no access to the sunlight, and no food.

The next day, anthrax was found in a letter mailed to NBC News. "Now tell me I'm crazy," I said to my husband, who had brought me a tuna sandwich at Ceramic City.

"I never said you were crazy," he said, wiping his lips with a napkin. "I'm just trying to say that if we're going to die, well . . ." He lifted his hands up, a gesture of acceptance.

"I can't," I said. "I can't just wait. Can you understand?"

My husband shook his head, his eyes full of sadness for me.

The CIPRONOW man said he would take a canoe and one hundred seventy-two dollars and sixteen cents. God knows why he wanted a canoe. Perhaps he had realized that the tide was turning: the government was in negotiations to buy a zillion tablets of discount Cipro, and the terrorists were hatching smallpox. The Cipro market was at peak performance.

Maybe he liked to fish, I don't know.

I gave the CIPRONOW man our address. He arrived with a Ziploc bag full of pills and a trailer for the canoe. I invited him inside for a beer and he accepted. I gave him a Shiner Bock. "This is a beautiful home," he said. He looked around, nodding. I saw it through his eyes: the books lined up in a row on the bookcase my husband had built for me, my copy of *To Lake N'Gami and Back* next to my husband's *Trout of the World.* The cat—once my cat, but now *ours*—curled up in a circle on the floor. The large glass windows, which could shatter with little provocation. The CIPRONOW man sipped his beer, and then looked down at his American flag shirt.

I got things ready for my husband: I made a seafood stew with coconut milk and lemongrass. I put out two green bowls we had bought at a tag sale. Next to the salt and pepper shakers, which were shaped like Hawaiian dancers, I placed the bag of Cipro pills. They looked good, as if they belonged.

After some time, when my husband had not come home, I poured a glass of wine and called my mother. "I saw Lou Kensington at the Yacht Club Christmas party," she confided. I could see my mother, leaning against the kitchen doorway in her New Canaan home. She twisted the phone cord around her finger, and although this habit had always seemed annoying, now it seemed precious, and I wished I had never moved away from her.

"Lou is not doing well," said my mother. "He's obsessed with where Howie was on the plane."

I finished my glass of wine and poured another. "Where was he?" I said. I tried to think reverentially of Howie Kensington, but the only vision I could summon was one of Howie in his football helmet, his face sweaty.

"Lou thinks he was bumped to first class, next to one of the terrorists. Howie called his girlfriend and told her he was going to order a free St. Pauli Girl, even though it was morning."

"I hope he did," I said.

"So do I," said my mother. After a minute, she said, "Howie was the captain of the hockey team at Yale."

"I know," I said.

"You wanted to go to Yale," said my mother, "but you didn't get in."

"I know," I said.

. . .

My husband had still not returned from the lab by the time I finished the wine and went to sleep. I wrote a note, and placed it on the kitchen table, next to the bag: "I hope you will understand that this is for us."

I do not remember my husband coming home: his long back, his thin eyelids, his mind full of numbers, his bottom, warm against my stomach. By the time I woke, he was out of bed again, and I was alone.

I found him, freshly showered, in the kitchen. The morning paper was still rolled up, bound by a rubber band. I went to the coffeepot and filled a china cup. My head pounded, and I was still in the dress I had worn to work the previous day.

On the table, my note was gone, and in its place was a box of condoms.

We sat opposite each other, the bag of pills and the box of condoms between us. The smell of coffee filled the kitchen. The sun cast a buttery light, and the hairs on my husband's forearm looked like gold.

## Butte as in Beautiful

It's a crappy coincidence that on the day James asks for my hand in marriage, there is a masturbator loose in the library. On Monday morning, for example, everything's the same. Pearl gets picked for the Copper Lunchbox, so we have to listen to Steve Winwood all afternoon. Rosie goes, "Did you have to pick all Steve Winwood?" and Pearl goes, "Look. It's my Copper Lunchbox."

"Fair enough," I say, and then I say, "Can you all be quiet so I can alphabetize in peace?"

Pearl and Rosie snort and turn up the radio. When you see a chance, take it. Find romance, make it make it.

We fight about the radio, primarily. We've each been

picked for Copper Lunchbox at least once, and then all the library patrons put down their newspapers (which they're not reading anyway) and think it's their job to comment on your musical tastes. They don't have real jobs in Butte anymore, so people take what they can get. In July, and it was hot, Old Ralph announced that Madonna's music heralded the final tear in America's moral fabric. I was like, "You know what, Old Ralph? Relax. 'Crazy for You' is a dance song, not a code of ethics." Old Ralph's like, "Touch me once and you know it's true. I never wanted anyone like this!" making the words sound lewd and disgusting. I almost took the new Mary Higgins Clark and beaned him, but Ralph likes to pontificate, and in a public library, that's his right.

So, we live in Butte, Montana. The richest hill on earth, ha, ha. They dug a pit the size of the city next to the city and now it's filling with toxic water. It'll overflow in the year 2000 they say, so I say, well, a year is a year. Now they're talking about mining the water.

My dad was a miner. He's dying now of cancer—it's in his bones—and all his friends are dying of cancer too. They come over to the house and drink Guinness and smoke like fiends and what's Mom going to say? It's bad for your health? When I get home, there's some kind of meat or some Beefaroni, and when I get in bed, my sheets smell like Downy. In between my dad's coughing, I can hear my mother's soft laughter.

They hired me at the library out of Butte High. I was the class valedictorian. At the graduation ceremony, I said, "Go forth and find your dreams." I could have gone to Missoula and played for the Lady Griz, but my coach was like, "Annie, that knee's going to give in less than a season." I had to tape it for the last game as it was, but the Lady Griz still wanted me. They are the best women's basketball team in Montana. They went to State and then to Florida to play in the championships this year. I watch them on TV. They're all as tall as me, with their hair in little ponytails, and they were on the beach with suntan lotion all over their noses because hey, they're from Montana and their skin isn't used to Florida sun. One of them married the quarterback of the Grizzly football team. She wore a cowboy hat with a veil, which I think is tacky.

So, people used to send their daughters to Butte because their skin would get pale here, and that was fashionable. The arsenic in the air will bleach your skin. Our Lady of the Rockies is white as snow.

Our Lady of the Rockies is a hundred-foot marble statue of the Virgin Mary. Butte bought her and helicoptered her up to the Continental Divide to give the town something to be proud of, when all the copper was gone. At night, with the moon over her shoulder, she is something out of a dream. No matter what goes wrong or crazy, staring at Our Lady of the Rockies makes me calm. She's right where she should be, and it's a good thing, because she weighs eighty tons.

After work, James picks me up and we go driving. Sometimes we drive over to Pork Chop John's for sandwiches, sometimes to the flats for a beer, and sometimes we go all the way out to Deer Lodge where the prison is or to Anaconda where the smokestack of the old smelter rises up like an arm.

James! He smells like hard work—a cinnamon, cigarette smell. When James started calling me, he had just dropped out of tenth grade. Butte is small; I knew who he was, of course, and that he lived with his deadbeat father in a drafty double-wide. Nobody thought it would last, the studious girl and the grocery guy with a tattoo of his dead mother on his back.

After work, James plays saxophone for the Toxic Horns. His hair always looks messy and sticks up like a little chick-adee. His tongue is the softest thing in the world.

Back to Monday. By the afternoon it's raining, and that's the best time to shelve. It's quiet and warm in the library, and the books are all organized and beautiful. I'm humming and checking out the Romance section when there's a shriek from the second floor. It's Pearl and she goes, "OH NOOOOO! AAAH!" and the upstairs exit slams shut and Pearl comes running down the stairs like a puppy. Her mascara is smudged and her wiglet is askew.

"What? What?" goes Rosie, and Pearl can't say it. She breathes in and out and finally she says, "There was a man upstairs."

A man? (All the librarians are spinsters or divorcées and hate men.) I was like, "Pearl, men are allowed to go wherever they—"

And Pearl goes, "NO! You don't UNDERSTAND!" And she starts crying. Rosie leads her by her little liver-spotted hand into the bookbinding room and Pearl's shoes make this shuffling sound. You can hear the two of them talking quietly and then Pearl's crying, Rosie's soothing sounds. A few minutes later, Rosie comes out. Her mouth is drawn together tight as a prune.

"There is a masturbator loose in the Periodical area," says Rosie.

By now all the regulars have dropped their newspapers. Nobody's even pretending to browse. Old Ralph (of course) leads the way. He runs up the stairs with determination on his face for the first time since I have known him. Abe follows him and the little biddies stand at the foot of the stairs chirping encouragement.

Nothing.

The masturbator had escaped. That afternoon, Rosie gets the whole story out of poor (Catholic as they come) Pearl. She had noticed a strange man in the Science periodicals. (I was like, "What was he reading? *Discover? Scientific American?*" but Rosie told me to zip my lips.) The man was tall with brown hair combed back. He had a receding hairline and was wearing jeans, a brown leather jacket, and white penny loafers.

So, Pearl's organizing the magazines, maybe reading a bit as she usually does, which is why it takes her forever and a day, and she hears sounds from the man. What sounds? Grunting sounds and breaths, little short ones. (Pearl kept saying, "Like a bear, like a bear," but nobody wanted to explore that statement.) So finally she looks up and his back's to her. He's hunched a bit.

You have to understand about Pearl. She's sixty-five, and her husband was brought over straight from County Galway. He was killed in a mine explosion, but not before he left Pearl for a stripper. She never remarried, or went on a date, or even talked a whole lot to a man after that. In short, the masturbator had to turn around, raise an eyebrow, and give Pearl an eyeful before she realized he was no regular library patron. She was paralyzed for a minute. According to Rosie, who appointed herself official psychoanalyst, he finished the job right there and then, and that is why Pearl doesn't use the water fountain anymore. Pearl finally screamed and came galloping down the stairs, and the masturbator escaped.

James drove past Pork Chop John's. He had showered, and didn't smell like his lunch-break Winstons but like Paco Rabanne. "What, did you leave work early?" I said.

He looked at me, and put his hand on my knee. "Annie," he said, "I did. I left work early today." He was talking like a movie, which pissed me off. There was a long, uncomfortable silence. Usually, we couldn't find enough to say to each other—what food must be like in foreign countries, why our parents failed, MTV. In summer, we lay in the bed of James's truck and made up stories of our bright future, our heads cradled by James's winter parka and snow pants.

While James was busy squeezing my knee, he missed the light on Mercury and almost ran into a hippie Volkswagen van. "Van!" I cried, and he hit the brakes in time. "I'm hungry," I said.

"Darling, you shall be fed," said James.

"I'm in an onion ring mood."

James shook his head. "So, James," I said, "a masturbator is loose in the library." James sighed.

"I don't want to talk about that," he said. He licked his lips. "Annie, if you could go anywhere, anywhere for dinner this evening, where would it be?"

I thought for a minute. "Tower Pizza," I said.

"No."

"Yes! You said I could choose, James. What's your problem?"

James was breathing hard and talking strangely. He was making me nervous. "Skip it," I said. "Mom's making meat loaf anyway."

"Fine!" yelled James, jerking the steering wheel and pulling into the parking lot. James didn't even touch his salad or the double pepperoni with mushrooms. He listened glumly as I told him about the masturbator.

Then, the moment. The moment went like this:

*Curtain opens on a young couple in Tower Pizza, an orange-walled restaurant with waxed yellow floors. The couple is smoking cigarettes and eating pizza from small plastic plates. The woman uses a knife and fork and the man uses his hands.*

ME: Should we have gotten extra cheese?

JAMES: No. This is fine.

ME: I sort of wish I had caught the masturbator.

JAMES: Why?

ME: At least it would be exciting, you know?

JAMES: Annie, I got a promotion today. I'm leaving pro-
   duce.

ME: Awesome! I wish we had extra cheese.

JAMES: I'm going to be manager of the meat counter. I
   almost have enough money to get us out of this place.
   This fucking place! I'm taking you to New York. We
   can stay with my cousin in Armonk, and then we'll
   move to the city.

ME: Can we get cheesy garlic sticks, babe?

JAMES: Annie, will you marry me?

So I said yes, and we went up to Our Lady of the Rockies
and had sex. James fell asleep, but I lay awake and gazed at
Our Lady. At night she's lit up like a Christmas tree, her arms
open to us all.

The next day, there are posters all around the library. They
say: CAUTION, PLEASE, THIS MAN MAY BE MASTURBAT-
ING IN THE PERIODICALS ROOM and then there's a picture
that Pearl drew of a man's face. It looks like a cartoon pig. I
tell Pearl and Rosie the signs might lead people to believe the
man should be left alone, but they look at me with their
brows furrowed and I zip it. Everyone is very upset about
masturbation going on in the library.

Jan and the Morning Crew keep making jokes about us
on the radio and repeating the description of the masturbator,
down to the penny loafers. All of a sudden everybody wants
to hang out at the library, and the books are in disarray. I can't
bear it.

After an hour, Rosie tells me I need a break. I tell her somebody's got to shelve the damn books. She puts her hand on my shoulder and says, "Honey, the books aren't going anywhere."

I call my mother and ask her to have breakfast with me. She wasn't awake when I left for work, and my father was coughing too hard to notice the ring on my finger. It was a thick gold ring with a diamond the size of a pencil eraser—James's grandmother's ring. She was a famous lounge singer who was given the ring by a movie star I can never remember the name of. It glitters and flashes around as I file the card catalog. Nobody notices when I slip out a side door.

My mom is waiting at the Squat and Gobble. She has ordered her tea and my creamy coffee, and is wearing a pillbox hat. When I come in, she looks up, and in the bright sunlight her face is lined and dry. Jesus, I think, she's an old biddy. Then I feel guilty and give her a big hug. And don't you know she sees that rock on my finger before I even sit down.

"Margaret Ann," she says, "is that what I think it is?"

I say, "Yes," and her eyes fill with tears.

"James is a good boy, he is," she says.

"I know."

We eat eggs and bacon, and my mother dabs at the corners of her lips between bites. She comes from a wealthy Irish family and never lets us forget it.

"James was promoted to the meat department," I say. She smiles. "He wants to leave Butte." Her smile widens. "How do I know if this is the right thing, Mom?"

"Do you love him?"

I think of James and his baby chick hair. "Yes."

"I loved your papa, too," says my mother, and she shakes her head slowly. "Thank goodness you'll get out of this town," she says. She looks through the window, and I look too. There are old cars glinting in the sun. A man with a beard leans against Frank's Pawn Shoppe and draws a circle with his toe. He has only one arm. A woman comes out of Terminal Meats holding her dinner wrapped in paper. Her face is rosy and her shoes are shiny and new. Her coat is lined in fake fur and she holds it closed with the hand not holding the meat. She nods at the one-armed man, who smiles tiredly. "Maybe you and James could go to Florida," says my mother. "Just like the Lady Griz."

"My knee is broken!" I yell, by mistake. My mother shuts up like a clam and her face goes even paler.

"I'm sorry," I say. My mother stares at her eggs. She looks like what she is: an old lady with a husband who has cancer in his bones. Her pillbox hat is faded and her lipstick creeps into the wrinkles around her mouth. She doesn't dab at her eyes but lets her cheeks get all wet, so they look like they're made of clay.

"Why aren't you happy for me?" I say. "This ring belonged to Marlon Brando!"

My mother meets my gaze. "I am happy," she says.

"Why don't you come with me?" I say. "Why don't you go instead of me? I don't care."

"Breakfast is my treat," she says, and I watch her count change from her purse. On impulse, I grab her soft fingers. She looks up, startled, but does not pull away.

The masturbator has already left by the time I return to the library. This time it was Mrs. McKim who saw him in the Newspaper Nook. He was working himself into a frenzy by the stacks. Mrs. McKim didn't get a gander at the whole package. She saw the leather jacket and the loafers and ran screaming before he even turned around. He had gotten away by the time the police arrived. "Secure all the doors!" the police say to us. Nobody shelves the whole afternoon, and the books are not in order on the cart. All the peepers who have started hanging around begin to pick up books, look at the covers, and then drop them somewhere else. I find a Young Adult novel in the Reference Room! That night, I can barely sleep. I have my mother tell James I'm too sick to go dancing. In bed, I listen to the sounds of my house: the clink of silverware going in drawers, the hum of the TV. The creakings of two old people moving around each other in the night.

The next day, I take the ring off and put it in my pocket. It's getting in the way. I'm at the counter when they come in: three little kids brandishing pens. "We," says the tallest one, throwing her shoulders back, "are the Future Problem Solvers of America." I recognize her—she's Katie, the grand-daughter of one of my dad's miner pals. She has black hair parted in the middle and combed behind her ears. She wears glasses, and through them, her eyes are wide and blue. I know Katie's mother, June, who dropped out of Butte High and drinks too much.

Another kid chimes in. "We are working on deforesta-tion," he says.

"Check the card catalog under 'forest' or 'woods,' " I say. The Future Problem Solvers of America look sheepish.

"We can't read," says Katie.

"No worries," I tell her. I spend all afternoon helping the kids. We find pictures of clear-cut forests and pictures of lush, green ones. We find pictures of log homes, and rugged men with axes. The FPS of A leave satisfied. They promise to return next week, when they will begin to cure cancer. When they open the library entrance, the late-afternoon sun makes Katie's hair shine.

I tell James I have the flu, and watch television with my father. I wrap myself in an old blue blanket and laugh so hard that my father tells me to shut my piehole.

By Thursday, things have settled down at the library. The masturbator has not returned, and James has stopped coming by and asking what's wrong, what's wrong.

I'll tell you what's wrong. It took me all day to get that library back in order. What's wrong? People and their ability to mess everything up. Disorder always increases. That's the rule, according to Einstein or whoever. Well, I'm no Einstein, but I'll tell you this: I tape my knee every day. It won't get worse, and that's a promise.

I like being a librarian. I like the peace and quiet, and the smell of old paper. I like listening to Old Ralph and paging through magazines. Each book is stamped with a history: who's read it and when. Who needed a renewal. Nowadays, everybody loves mysteries, but I can prove that people used to like history books.

My kids are going to know all about history. Pocahontas

to Columbus to Marcus Daly, who took all the copper out of Butte and left us with his empty mansion and a cancer pond. I'm going to teach them to be a part of history, like the Lady Griz and their championship. Like the masturbator, even.

At three or so P.M., I hear the front door open. It makes a click sound and by the time I turn around, someone is climbing the stairs. I know without seeing that it's him. But I keep filing for a time. Really, I don't know what's the matter with me. Finally, when nobody else goes about catching him, I climb the staircase. It's a wooden staircase, and it makes a creaking sound with each step. Outside the door to the Periodicals area, it's silent, and smells like chicken soup. I push on the door, and of course, there he is, the masturbator, whacking away.

"Hey!" I say, and he turns around. His face is red. His hair is neatly combed, and his shirt is white and pressed. He looks like somebody's lawyer, or somebody's dad. Granted, his dick is hard and he's got his meaty hand around it. But the expression on his face is not panic. He looks relieved, or like I had walked in with a present all tied up in a bow. He says, "Oh."

What is there for me to do? I am eighteen years old, and a grown man is standing between me and the weekly periodicals and he's got his pants unzipped. I am a librarian, and a Montanan.

I recognize the look in his eyes.

"Go home," I tell him. "Can't you just go home?" And something changes in his face. His eyes fill up with tears.

Rosie comes through the door. She has been fixing her

hair and she smells like Aqua Net and a new dose of perfume. Her mouth opens wide, and she grabs me. The man (dick completely soft by this time, and swinging wildly) pushes us to the ground and heads for the door. Old Ralph tackles him downstairs, and when the cops arrive, the masturbator is tied to the card catalog with packing tape.

It turns out that the masturbator has a name: Neil Davidson. He lives in Helena with his wife and two kids. He's a mortgage broker. His picture is on the front page of the Friday paper, along with my name and the name of our library. It is an old picture: his hair is thick, and he wears a tie. His smile is full of hope.

"What a sick, sick man," says my mother, looking at the paper over my shoulder. Her hair is still pinned in curls, and she has given me my toast with honey. She is rotting from the inside, I can smell it.

"You got that right," calls my father from the living room. His oxygen tube almost drowns out the television. I can see my father's face, and it is gray and resentful.

I don't say anything, but I know they are wrong. I saw Joseph Davidson in the flesh. I knew the look in his eyes. I wish my parents would just be quiet. I will call James today, and I will give him back his ring. "Please understand, James," I will say. And then I will tell him what I should have told the masturbator: There are plenty of things worse than having a home, and doing what you have to do to stay there.

# The Stars Are Bright in Texas

They told us the baby was dead, and two days later we were on a plane to Texas. We were moving, and had to buy a house. We'd always rented, and all our furniture was from Goodwill. We'd never had a realtor before. We were going to be rich.

In my carry-on bag, I had three magazines, an apple, and two bottles of prescription pills: an antibiotic and a painkiller. I swallowed one pill from each bottle as we taxied down the runway, leaving Bloomington, and my dead baby, behind.

It hadn't even been a baby, my doctor said, despite my morning sickness, tender breasts, and anticipatory purchases from A Pea in the Pod. It was just a mass of cells, the wrong egg fertilized. Though my husband, Greg, knew more than any of us about chromosomal abnormalities, he was superstitious—he was convinced it was because he was drunk or stressed out from his pharmaceutical company interviews when we conceived. That night had been a heavenly memory: the smell of a fire, snow falling quietly outside our bedroom window. Now it was just a storm and a mistake.

We landed at George Bush Intercontinental Airport. Joe, from Lone Star Realty, picked us up in his mother-in-law's gold minivan. He wore a Mexican wedding shirt that would be soaked through by the end of the day.

Our friends Daniel and Jane had recommended Lone Star Realty. Daniel finished his PhD in molecular biology a year before Greg, and we watched with fascination as he went through the recruiting process. When Daniel slipped his wrists into the golden handcuffs, which was what we called pharmaceutical jobs, he and Jane went to Texas for a weekend and returned with stories of giant houses, hot brisket, and a dip called *queso*. Daniel, too, had considered a teaching job, but PharmaLab's glittering promises were too wonderful to resist. "Once you're in, you never get out," mused Daniel, who had shaved his grad-school beard for interviews, revealing a small, pale chin.

"But why would you want to?" Jane asked. "Did we tell you we're getting four thousand square feet? And a flipping pool! We're twenty-six." She shook her head with wonder.

"I'm twenty-eight," I said.

"See what I'm saying?" she replied, gesturing at our dumpy Bloomington apartment, where I had just microwaved us two mugs of Earl Grey. Daniel and Jane were away the weekend we visited Houston, but promised to throw us a pool party when we arrived for good.

I tried to ignore the way Joe's hands shook, the fact that he took a wrong turn getting to the first house, and then said, "Hey, now this is cute!" as if he'd never visited the neighborhood before. We were looking at houses in the Woodlands, the planned community north of Houston where Pharma-Lab was located. We could live in a real city, Daniel had told us, but the commute would be a bitch.

The first house was on Pleasure Cove Drive. It was made of limestone, and had an orange roof. The "country kitchen" included a wood-paneled refrigerator, and the nursery was furnished from the same Pottery Barn Kids catalog I had on my bedside table. This mother had chosen the Lullaby Rocker and Ottoman in cranberry twill. I had wanted butter twill.

"Did you see the country kitchen?" asked Joe. "How about the master suite?" He seemed overly excited.

The master suite had pictures of Chicago sports teams all over one wall. A wedding photo featured a blonde with a dazzling smile. The husband was not such a looker, but hey. Someone was reading *Who Moved My Cheese?* in bed. The other one was reading *Star*.

Greg was in the yard, under a sign that said MARGARI-TAVILLE!

"I hate it," I said.

"Oh," he said, "okay." We moved toward the minivan.

·   ·   ·

As we drove to another house, Joe chatted with himself. "Silly flooring choices," he said, and "tiles from the wrong period." He turned on Treasure Cove Drive and stopped in front of a faux Victorian. "Right," he said, running a hand through his hair. He told us the price of the house, which was one hundred thousand more dollars than we could afford, even with the handcuffs.

I looked back at Greg, who shrugged. He was wearing a light blue shirt I had sewn for him—it was the color of his eyes. He had a fresh haircut, and looked weary but optimistic.

My brother, Adam, a devotee of HGTV, would have loved the house on Treasure Cove. It was solid brick—so unlike the house we had grown up in, which shook during Georgia thunderstorms—and had a media room with a wet bar and a giant deck for entertaining.

I was feeling woozy and dreamy. In a stranger's bathroom, I changed my Maxi Pad. The bathroom had a Jacuzzi tub. I wrapped the old pad in toilet paper and stuck it in my pocket. My blood—which had cushioned the mass of cells—dripped into the toilet bowl. In the tub, someone had lit berry-scented candles. I began to feel ill. I took a few breaths, then composed myself and joined my husband, who was admiring the skylight above the bed. A stitched pillow proclaimed THE STARS ARE BRIGHT IN TEXAS. It was a mass-produced piece of junk. Perhaps no one had the time to hand-stitch in Houston. Perhaps no one had a motto worth hand-stitching. THE HOUSES ARE BIG IN TEXAS, I thought. THE HAIR IS BLOND IN TEXAS. WHAT AM I DOING IN TEXAS?

In the minivan, I said I was too tired to trek around any-more. "Sweetie," said Greg, "we only have this weekend. . . ."

"How about a Diet Dr Pepper?" suggested Joe. "Got a twelve-pack in the cooler."

My empty womb was starting to cramp. "I just don't feel so well," I said. "I'm on antibiotics."

Joe smoothly put the car in gear. He talked about strep throat, how he always used to get strep throat as a kid, always taking antibiotics.

"Let's hit a few more houses," said my husband. "Kimmy, you rest in the car. I'll let you know if anything's amazing." The doctor had suggested we cancel the trip, but I had al-ready covered my shifts, and I wanted so much to fly some-where new, somewhere else, and buy a home. Our apartment was grimy, despite the curtains I had made from vintage fab-ric. The previous tenants had left old pots and pans; there was even a towel in the bathroom that said RANDY.

"You'll be completely wiped out after the procedure," the doctor had said, as I lay on a gurney, an IV in my arm. I was given an anti-nauseal called Regulan.

"I feel a bit weird already," I said.

"Hm," said the doctor, leaning in. I was her first operation of the day: I could smell the hair dryer and Aqua Net. "Do you feel anxious, jittery, like you want to jump off the table?"

"I do."

"It's the Regulan," said the doctor, matter-of-factly. But I was also about to go into surgery, to have what was left of my baby scraped out. We had prematurely named the baby Madeline or Greg Junior.

"You'll be in la la land in a sec anyway," said the doctor.

She was right. The next thing I knew, a nurse said, "It's all over. Now don't forget Doc's instructions."

She pulled back a white curtain, and there was Greg, his eyes red. "Mouse," he said, and he tried to smile.

The nurse continued, "Dr. O'Brien told you the surgery was fine, and you asked when you could have a margarita."

"What did she say?" Greg and I asked in unison.

"She said Sunday."

It was Friday night when Joe dropped us at the Hilton Garden Inn, but we ordered margaritas anyway at the Great American Grill. The espadrilles I had bought for the trip were already giving me blisters. We were depressed.

"I can't imagine myself in any of these McMansions," I said, poking an ice cube with my straw.

"I'm not hungry, but I'm getting fried chicken," said Greg.

"I miss it," I said. Greg slid his chair next to mine and took me in his arms.

"I know," he said. "Me too."

Three nights before, I had climbed into bed and said, "I have a little blood in my underwear."

"What?"

"But I looked on the Internet. Something about old blood, sometimes, like making room for the growing uterus or something. I don't know." I felt a sick excitement, speculating that I'd get some extra attention and maybe see the baby on an early sonogram, paid for by Blue Cross/Blue Shield.

"It's probably nothing," Greg had said, putting one hand on my stomach and the other on his fruitfly genome data.

After two rounds of margaritas, we went to our hotel room. Greg took a shower and joined me in bed, smelling of the hotel's ginger citrus shampoo. When he fell asleep, I was alone in a humid city.

I was six when a man approached my mother near the perfume counter at Dillard's. Once in a while, she took us shopping in Atlanta, about an hour from our hometown of Haralson, Georgia, population 143. The man asked my mother if she'd ever thought of being a model. She laughed in a way I had never heard, showing her throat. She said she was happily married with two small children. The man told my mother they had nannies in Paris, who were called au pairs.

In my memory, the man had dark hair and shiny skin. He wore a suit and tie. He handed her a card and said, "Just promise me you'll *think* about it." My mother was a rare beauty, he said.

She looked at the card, her forehead creased. She said, "I'll think about it. Okay, I will, I'll think about it." She bought a shirt for my brother and a plaid jumper for me, and then she drove us home.

She was beautiful, my mother. She'd rest her long, bare arms on her knees and stare into space while I tried to capture her attention. She didn't cook, like other mothers, or put name tags in my clothes. I can imagine her hanging my new dress in my closet, mulling her options. Did she even hesitate? Lighting a cigarette, dialing the number, packing her suitcase.

I don't know if she made it to Paris, or became famous there. Whatever she found, I hope it brought her happiness. I hope it was better than my brother and me.

At ten the next morning, I climbed into the front seat of Joe's mother-in-law's minivan. Greg was in the back, next to the cooler. We drove south, heading into a neighborhood I loved immediately. There was a big park with a swimming pool, and a jungle gym surrounded by moms holding take-out coffees.

"Okeydokey," said Joe, looking through a messy pile of papers, each a possible place for us to live. "Okay, now," he said, "we're a few blocks from the Ginger Man, a good little bar."

Greg and I locked eyes happily.

We walked into the house, and it was perfect. High ceilings, a big open kitchen for me to cook in, or learn to cook in. A bonus craft room, where I could put the Singer sewing machine my father had given me when I graduated from college three years before. I found Greg in a second garden, off the bedroom. He stood with his hands on his hips, gazing up at the canopy of trees. When I approached, he turned and looked at me.

"We found it," I said.

"I could love this," he agreed quietly.

"Yes," I said. My mind swam with visions of us: reading the paper on the front step, walking across the street with towels slung around our necks, tucking someone into bed in the kids' room. I opened the freezer and saw ice-cream sandwiches. I thought, *I love ice-cream sandwiches.*

Maybe it was the caffeine—which I was drinking for the first time in months—but the next few houses were a blur. We chattered about mortgages and contracts. As Joe drove, I furnished the house in my mind: a sleek couch in front of the fireplace—maybe leather? I imagined myself in the craft room, sliding fabric under the needle, really making a go of Madeline Designs, now that I no longer had to waitress every night.

Joe's cell phone rang. "Hello?" he said. "No, no," he said. "Couldn't have been me." He snapped the phone shut and turned to look at us. "Somebody took the key to the first house. That was the owner. He's pissed." He shook his head and chuckled.

I looked at Greg, who said coldly, "Why don't you check your pockets, Joe."

Joe's phone rang again. "What?" he said. He started to flush. "Well, okeydokey," he said. "I-I-I . . ." He stopped talking and nodded, then closed the phone. "I guess we're the only ones who've been there. But I just don't—"

"Watch out for the divider," said Greg in a steely voice.

As we doubled back to all the houses we'd seen, I tried to calm my husband. "It's going to be perfect," I said, as he muttered, "total waste of our time." After Joe found the key to

our dream house, locked in another house, he called the owners. "Hi there, Joe Jones, Lone Star Realty," he said. "The
funniest thing—"

"Don't turn on University," said Greg from the backseat.
Joe turned on University. We sat in traffic caused by a construction site—a site we had driven by earlier—in complete
silence.

By lunchtime, we had returned the key. The house looked
better than ever. A lemonade stand had been set up by the
park. A little boy rode by on his bicycle, a wrapped birthday
present in the basket.

Joe took us out to lunch. I popped my pills right at the
table and changed my Maxi Pad in the bathroom. I was not
healthy. I ate a cheeseburger with avocado, cheddar, and
bacon. I called my father in Haralson and said, "We found
it," and my father said, "That's wonderful, Kimmy."

Across the restaurant, Greg spoke excitedly into his cell
phone. "Mom," he said, "Listen to this, Mom . . ."

Over lunch, we filled out the paperwork, making an offer for
full price and then some. Joe assured us we would get the
house. Between bites of his burrito, Joe told us he had just hit
his stride at Enron when the shit storm hit. "Thought I'd give
this real estate thing a try," he said. He talked about his six-
month-old baby, whom he called "Girly." His wife, also an
Enron-employee-turned-realtor, he called "Doll."

After lunch, we drank Diet Dr Pepper and looked at
many houses that sucked, feeling superior.

That night, I wore a strapless dress. It was deep green,

and had a matching jacket with three-quarter-length sleeves. We wandered around the Woodlands, trying to find a restaurant where we could splurge, though we were nervous about spending every cent PharmaLab had promised and hundreds of thousands they hadn't. If we got the house, we could no longer say, "Oh, screw Big Pharma. Let's just move to Wyoming and live off the land."

Though we were outside, I felt as if we were trapped in a mall, with one neon-lit shop after another. All we could find was a Cheesecake Factory, and I've never liked cheesecake, so we returned to the Great American Grill.

"Cheers," I said, holding my margarita high.

Greg brought his glass to mine, and said, "Cheers, my love." We toasted ourselves, and the little family we would begin, as soon as I was no longer bleeding heavily. A week before, I had packed some Victoria's Secret Supermodel Sexy Whipped Body Cream into my suitcase. It would keep.

The gold minivan pulled up as usual in the morning, but Joe was no longer at the wheel. Instead, Doll—whose real name was Sally—hopped out. She was short and plump, her red hair in barrettes. "Joe wanted a day with the baby, and I needed some adult time," Sally explained. Her skirt was tight and orange, and she wore plastic jelly sandals. As we sipped coffee and ate bagels, Sally's phone rang. It appeared her phone was broken, and she could use only the speaker attachment.

With Girly crying in the background, Joe told Sally that there was another offer on our dream house. We needed to name our best price right now, he said, and the owners would decide in the next five minutes.

I felt flustered. The next five minutes? Neither Joe nor Sally knew whether we should raise our price or not. "They could have a lowball offer," said Sally. She added, "Or they could have a higher offer." She took a bite of her bagel. "Yum," she said.

Greg had done some calculations on his laptop (he loved Excel spreadsheets) and concluded the house was worth less than the asking price. We decided to hold firm, and headed out with a list of addresses, waiting nervously for Sally's phone to ring. "Might as well keep looking, just in case," said Sally. The flight back to our rental apartment and my dog-eared copy of *What to Expect When You're Expecting* was at 4 P.M.

On Scullers Cove Court, we entered an airless house where someone collected Hummel figurines. "This would be a great house for an older couple with no kids," mused Sally. She stood in the hallway, telling us about Girly, and how she didn't like tummy time, but how Sally had to make her do her tummy time. It was so stressful, said Sally.

Back in the minivan, we parked outside another (gigantic) house. "Whoops!" said Sally. "Y'all? It looks like I locked my purse inside that other house? And my phone's in it, and my Palm. And it's locked, oh, whoops! And we can't look at any other houses, cause my realtor key is also—"

"In your purse," Greg finished.

Sally thought fast. "How about I drop y'all off for a nice

lunch?" she suggested. "And I'll go get all this worked out? And y'all can have a real nice lunch?"

"It's ten-thirty," I said. "I don't want lunch. Our flight leaves in a few hours!" I was a wreck, admittedly.

"Oh, whoops," commented Sally.

At the hotel concierge desk, Sally made some calls. Greg stared at his nice new shoes. The night before, we had made each other crack up by saying, "Diet Dr Pepper!" and "Girly!" Now, nothing seemed so hilarious.

Sally finished her whispered calls and approached, looking a little less spry. Again, she made the case for an early lunch.

"What about the house?" said Greg loudly.

"Oh, right," said Sally. "I did talk to Joe. We lost the house. But how about I run get my keys, and . . . a nice, you know, lunch?"

I listened vaguely as Greg discussed the situation further, learning that we had been outbid, and it was over, though we could make a backup offer. When the calls were made and what phones worked and where various keys ended up, we were too exhausted to clarify. I would never stand in that beautiful kitchen, eating an ice-cream sandwich in my bathing suit.

I went upstairs and changed my Maxi Pad and swallowed my pills. I took off my oversize sunglasses and lay down. Reflexively, I put my hands on my stomach, but then remembered, and let them fall open.

We spent a long afternoon looking at other homes. We

tried to convince ourselves that a too-small house with a crazy water feature was even better, all things considered, but as Sally dropped us off at the airport, a sinking feeling was already settling in.

"Don't forget," said Sally, as I climbed from the van, "the perfect home is out there."

"Okay," I said. Four days before, a technician had moved her wand on my skin and looked at an image on the screen. The doctor was sure everything was fine. The ultrasound was just a precaution. Greg told me he could see the baby's face—its eyes—but when the doctor explained that the baby had never grown more than a few weeks old, that it had no head, and no heart, Greg said he must have been wrong.

In two weeks, my baby, the mass of cells, would be analyzed and we would be told it was tetraploidy. The doctor wrote something on her rectangular pad, then handed it to me. The paper read, "Tetraploidy. 92, XX, YY."

"Any questions?" asked the doctor.

I knew that to Greg, these symbols would mean something, bloom into a narrative. To me, they were cruel and unfathomable. "But why?" I said. "What did I do?"

She sighed, and said, "Nothing, Kimberly. It had absolutely nothing to do with you. It's just . . . the way things work out sometimes." She scribbled again, handing me a prescription for Prozac. When I got back to our apartment, I put both sheets of paper in my underwear drawer.

Outside the Houston airport, Greg waited, holding our bags. He stood, broad shoulders a little slumped, and watched me.

I remembered the sweet shock I'd felt when I'd first seen him, in the audience of my graduation fashion show. Most of my classmates, like Greg's sister, presented glamorous gowns, but I designed coats for little girls, swinging cape-style coats made of wool and fastened with vintage toggles. I knitted matching scarves and mittens. I'd worn only plastic parkas growing up—my designs came from my imagination, and a picture I'd seen once of a Parisian schoolgirl, standing in front of the Arc de Triomphe. Though the SCAD store had wanted to buy my whole collection, I saved one red coat, one scarf, one set of mittens.

"Have a safe trip home," said Sally.

"Okay," I said. I walked to my husband, and he folded me inside his arms. I wanted to say something, to fix something. He looked so young, and so bewildered.

"I can't believe it," I said. "It happened so fast."

"There will be another," he said.

We looked at each other. There would be another, there would. But I wanted the one that was gone.

# On Messalonskee Lake

## ONE

A woman had drowned in the lake, but that did not make it any less picturesque. We hadn't known her, after all; I had never met her, and my husband, Bill, was a boy when she died. She was Bill's aunt Renée, married to his father's brother, Gerry. She played the violin. This was all I could get out of my husband during our drive up I-95.

"So she fell out of the boat?" I said, waddling into the cabin, which smelled of either pine, Pine-Sol, or both.

"Yeah," said Bill.

"When was this?"

"A while ago," said Bill. "I told you, I was just a kid."

"Jesus," I said.

"We need some air," said Bill. He was wandering around, opening doors and windows.

"Who falls out of a boat?" I said. "It's very sad."

My husband approached. He tried to take me in his arms, but I barely fit. "Here," I said, pressing his palm to my stomach. His fingers were warm, and I leaned into him.

"What?" he said, into my hair. He moved his thumb along my neck softly; I kissed him.

"I think it's hiccuping," I said. There was a bubbling sensation inside me, not the kicks I had come to know, but something lighter.

"Maybe it's laughing," said my husband.

When we realized we would never be alone again, Bill and I had decided on a romantic week at his family's Maine cabin. He had spent his childhood at Camp Snow Island, and I knew he wanted to move back and run it someday. Unless I was hit by a bus or got trigger toe, I wasn't leaving the Boston Ballet, but I was happy to spend a week in the wilderness.

I asked for an economy car when I called Thrifty Rental, but when we took our key into the parking lot, there was a PT Cruiser in Slot A-8. "No," said Bill, when he saw it.

"I think it's cute," I said.

"You cannot drive a PT Cruiser to Belgrade Lakes," said my husband. "You can't step out of that car and buy bait."

"I'll buy the bait," I said.

"Lord help us all," said my husband.

. . . .

I began putting away the groceries we'd bought on the way: jam, bread, milk, eggs. "Was Renée pretty?" I asked, opening the refrigerator.

"Sure," said Bill. "I don't know." He motioned to one of the family photos placed around the cabin in tarnished frames. "There she is," he said.

I peered at the photograph. Aunt Renée wore a bemused expression and a bandanna. She had her hand on the shoulder of a little boy. "Who's that?" I said. "I thought you said they didn't have kids."

"That's me," said Bill.

"Oh," I said. The boy in the picture—Bill—was smiling timidly. I wondered if our baby would be shy.

At Day's General Store, we bought steaks and beer. I had gained eighteen pounds, but the doctor told me to eat even more. He wasn't really worried, he said, but he was cautiously concerned. Jocelyn, who was in my company, hadn't gained enough pregnancy weight, and her baby was born six weeks early. Little Allan was fine, but the story was scary enough to make me choke down a bunch of beef.

As Bill manned the grill, I sat on the deck overlooking Messalonskee Lake. Snow Island, where the camp was located, was faintly visible across the water. A green boat puttered by: a man and his young daughter. "Any luck?" called my husband, and the girl held up a fish.

"Goddamn," said Bill. He was in his element here, a fact I tried to forget every morning as he set his jaw and stepped on the T, uncomfortable in a suit and tie. Bill didn't like cities in general and Boston in specific. He loathed his job raising money for the Appalachian Trail Society. I had studied dance in Burlington, Vermont, for the first few years of our marriage. We had planned on a lifetime of dreaming big and working hard. When I actually made it, we were both ecstatic, but also stunned.

"I can't wait to take the boat out," said Bill.

"Is it the same boat?" I asked. "The one Renée fell out of?"

"What?" said Bill. "Maybe, but I doubt it."

I hefted myself out of the chair—my balance was completely off now—and walked across the pine needles to take a peek. It was yellow, with a bucket in the stern.

Bill finished grilling, and we ate at a wooden picnic table. We made up two beds on the screen porch and lay in one. Bill pressed his ear to my belly, trying—but failing—to hear a heartbeat. I pulled my maternity tank top up, feeling his scratchy cheek against my skin.

For days, we napped and cooked and swam in the lake. I worked out regularly—I was expected back in the studio six weeks after the baby was born, so there was no time for a break. In my off-time, I constructed elaborate stories about dead Renée: a doomed affair, a clandestine meeting gone disastrously wrong. I pressed Bill for details, but he claimed to know nothing. Had he been there the night she drowned? He was asleep, he said. Was she depressed? How would I know, he said. He told me not to get worked up. Each evening, the man and his daughter floated past us, holding up lines of fish. Bill had some luck, and I even went with him a few times, though I joked I would sink the boat. I loved watching my husband paddle—the movement of his strong muscles.

On our last night at the cabin, we sat on the deck as the sun set. The baby performed *petit allegros* in my womb, and Bill held my hand. Suddenly, he stood up and pulled off his shirt, then his pants. "Lovebug, what are you doing?" I said. Naked, Bill stretched and smiled. Then he did a swan dive into the freezing—even in summer—water. He emerged a few feet out, like an otter.

"Join me?" he said.

"Oh, hon," I said, "I don't know."

He waited, expectant, and I decided it wasn't too much to ask.

The water felt thick and cool. It surrounded me, and then I surfaced, sputtering. I could smell algae. Bill watched me as I swam breaststroke. I reached my husband and wrapped myself around him the best I could.

After our impromptu swim, the baby was hungry, so I dressed and wandered into the kitchen. I ended up staring at every family photo until I found another of Renée. In this picture, she was standing next to Uncle Gerry, who had attended our wedding, and given us a salad bowl.

Gerry's hair was white now, but in the picture, it was reddish brown. He looked about nineteen. He and Aunt Renée were sitting side by side, wearing bathing suits. Renée held her hair back from her face; she squinted against a summer sun.

At our wedding, Uncle Gerry took me for a spin around the dance floor. He was still handsome, like Bill's dad, but the word was that he lived all alone somewhere in Canada. "You have everything in front of you," he said. His eyes were kind. "I'm jealous," he said.

"Can I call you Uncle Gerry?" I had asked.

He looked more bewildered than touched, but then the band began to play Van Morrison's "Into the Mystic." Bill came from behind and took me in his arms.

I brought the photo of Renée and Gerry outside. "Look at them," I said.

Bill sighed.

"They were happy, too," I said.

The sun's final rays shot across the lake, and the green boat came into view. I watched my husband as the girl and her father moved past. They waved, and Bill waved back. I knew that soon, I would no longer be the love of his life.

## TWO

There were tears and lists and bottles of frozen, yellow milk, but finally Bill was alone with his wife. She sat in the passenger seat of the rental car clutching her breast pump. "I just wish the cabin had a phone," said Lizzy.

Bill pulled out of his parents' driveway. "The baby," he said, "is fine." He felt as if he had been repeating these four words incessantly since Aurora's birth.

"I know," said Lizzy. "But do you think the cell will work?"

"My parents know where to find us," said Bill. "Can you try to relax?"

"To be honest," said Lizzy, "I don't want to go. I'm sorry, Bill, but I just don't. There—I said it."

Bill pressed on the accelerator. It was early fall, the trees still holding their auburn leaves. If Lizzy just stopped talking, they'd be at the cabin in an hour.

"Bill? Seriously. Let's just go another time."

"How about a donut?" said Bill, pointing to Kaye's Donuts, on the side of the road.

"A donut?" said Lizzy. She rubbed her eye with the heel of her hand. She was tired, of course, but so was he. At eighteen months old, Aurora still slept with Lizzy, waking a few times a night.

"Yes," he said. "A donut."

She gazed out the window. "Well," she said quietly, "okay."

"Just skip it," said Bill. "Just forget it."

"No, I want one," said Lizzy. "I want a donut, Bill. Maybe raspberry jelly?"

"It's too late," said Bill. He drove on.

It all began with a broken leg. Lizzy had returned to the company six weeks after Aurora's birth, and Bill loved pushing the baby to day care in the expensive stroller her parents had sent from Bennington. His job was a chore, but it paid the bills (as the Boston Ballet didn't) and he could often sneak out early to pick up his daughter.

Aurora was nine months old when she fell off a climbing gym at the park. Her scream was horrible, and her leg was broken in two places. Lizzy was dancing Odette in a *Swan Lake* matinee, and could not be reached. *What the hell were you doing?* she wanted to know, later that night, after she had given Aurora a sponge bath. Well, he had been reading *Portland Magazine* on a bench, sipping a latte. Bill agreed with his wife: it was his fault.

Aurora began protesting when Lizzy dropped her at Happy Baby Day Care, holding on to Lizzy and wailing. "I want to be with her," said Lizzy, calling Bill's cell phone, "and she wants to be with *me*." The last "me" was infused with a desperate, high-pitched tone.

They decided Bill would do the drop-off and the pickup. Lizzy would do the evening bath, the singing, the snuggling, the nighttime feeding. She would settle Aurora between them in bed and then say, "Bill, no. Not in front of the baby." She would sleep with Aurora held to her breast, and Bill would lie awake, move onto the couch, and do the drop-off and the pickup.

As they neared the cabin, Lizzy seemed calmer. They drove into the town of Belgrade Lakes, stopped at Day's for supplies. Bill slipped a bottle of wine into the basket, and Lizzy said, "It's for you, not me."

"You could have a glass. . . ."

"I don't want one."

"Then it's for me," said Bill. He tossed in a six-pack of Shipyard Ale. Lizzy added an apple. Bill picked out two steaks, and Lizzy found green beans. Bill got eggs and butter, and Lizzy brought the basket to the counter and placed a *People* magazine and a pack of gum on top. Bill paid.

When they reached the cabin, Bill found the key under an empty flowerpot, unlocking the door and breathing in the familiar smell of the musty kitchen. He felt a rush of well-being, a sense that anything was possible. He walked to the back porch, where he could see the lake. He could also see Lizzy, who was standing amidst the trees, trying to find cell phone reception. A leaf fell from a sugar maple, landing in her hair.

One morning, when Aurora was a year old, Lizzy had stopped packing her dance bag and sat down heavily at the kitchen counter. "Hon, coffee?" said Bill, pouring into a plastic travel mug.

Lizzy was in tights and a leotard, her hair uncombed. Aurora wandered around the kitchen, trying out her new purple shoes. She held up one foot and then the other, delighted. "I don't want to do this anymore," said Lizzy.

Bill sighed. "Hon, coffee?" he repeated.

"I won't take her to that filthy day care."

"We can't afford for me to leave my job," said Bill.

"I know," said Lizzy, her expression sad and sure. "I'm quitting the company."

"That's insane!" cried Bill.

Insane or not, she did it, returning home that afternoon with the contents of her locker and a pizza.

In Uncle Gerry's cabin, Bill opened the bottle of wine and poured a glass. Lizzy came inside and said, "Well! Your parents say Aurora's okay, but she hasn't even had her nap yet." She looked at Bill and his glass of wine, then went into the bedroom. "I'm going to lie down," she called.

"Great," said Bill.

It was early afternoon. Bill refilled his glass and walked down to the lake. He had hoped, without the baby and the city, that things could be different. Bill remembered bringing Lizzy to camp for the first time, expertly piloting their Whaler to Snow Island. He'd idled next to the old dock and jumped off with the rope, securing the boat and then holding out his hand for Lizzy, radiant in a blue sundress and white sneakers, her hair loosed from her usual bun.

"Oh, I get it," Lizzy had said, taking his hand and stepping elegantly across the narrow ribbon of water separating the boat from the dock. "This is who you are, Bill Ferris."

It began to rain softly as Bill finished the second glass of wine and climbed into the yellow boat. He had always loved the paddle to Ashworth Island, located at the far end of Messalonskee Lake. As a teenager, Bill had supervised all the camp trips to Ashworth, from the Minnows' first campout to the Sturgeons' Maine Woodsman Certification Exams, during which the eldest boys had to construct their own shelters, forage for and cook their food, and take exams on axmanship and fire construction.

Thunder cracked, but Bill was undeterred. He slid the boat into the water and began to row, chanting the list of local fish: *Black crappie, brook trout, brown trout, eel*—he switched sides, ignoring the rain—*bullhead, pickerel, chub, alewife. Three-spine stickleback, four-spine stickleback. Largemouth bass, smallmouth bass. Shiner, splake, pike, sucker. Pumpkinseed sunfish, redbreast sunfish. Smelt, salmon, white and yellow perch. Slimy sculpin, slimy sculpin!*

His father had taught him the roll long ago, though Bill wasn't even sure it was correct. He was no marine biologist. He hadn't even finished his English degree at UVM. He met Lizzy, she auditioned with the Boston Ballet, she was granted a spot in the company, and they moved.

Lizzy was an anxious mother; she could talk for twenty minutes about baby-proofing. (Sometimes, after a long day, Bill was too tired to deal with the KidCo toilet seat lock and just peed into the tub.) She seemed to have no regrets about leaving her life's work, no interest in movies or current events, no desire to put on makeup. Sometimes Bill looked at his wife and couldn't figure out what the fuck had happened.

But Aurora: at naptime, she slept on her stomach with her diaper in the air, her feet crossed underneath her. She was curious, earnest, her teeth tiny pearls. When she ran to Bill and settled herself perfectly against him, her head smelled like sunscreen and caramel.

He made it to Ashworth Island and climbed out of the

boat, pulling it to shore. He remembered camping on the island, jamming his legs into his L.L. Bean sleeping bag. Bill missed his child-size camp bag, navy with a black stripe. He'd been asleep inside it the night his aunt went missing.

Bill sat by the water, thinking about Aunt Renée's long-ago disappearance. Uncle Gerry had driven the roads of Belgrade Lakes, calling to check in from every pay phone he came across. When Bill's father, searching with a flashlight, realized the boat was gone, they all assumed—they prayed—she'd gotten lost out on the lake. The police dredged the water, and found Aunt Renée's body. At the funeral, Gerry sat next to the open casket, reaching inside to cover Renée's hand with his own.

Aunt Renée had always insisted on getting up early with Bill and his sisters, letting Bill's parents sleep in. She sat by the side of the lake in her bathrobe and played the violin while they chased each other and gathered twigs. Bill remembered the smell of blueberry pancakes and bacon, Renée's bow resting on the windowsill while she cooked. She was from some Midwestern city—Chicago?—but Gerry had brought her to Maine and she had stayed. Bill's clearest memory of his aunt was when she'd run after their car as they pulled out of the driveway. It was the end of Bill's family's summer visit, and Aunt Renée made Bill's mother stop and roll down the window. "I have one more kiss for the kids," she'd said. She blew them each a kiss and then stood alone in the road as they drove away, hugging her cardigan around her skinny frame.

The sky was red and gold as Bill paddled back. By the time the cabin came into view, it was nearly dark. In the evening light, he saw Lizzy's faint outline. She was sitting on the deck with her magazine. Bill remembered arriving at the studio to pick Lizzy up for dinner once, seeing her in the midst of practice. Across a mirrored room, bleached with overhead lights, Lizzy had leapt and landed, the muscles in her thighs as solid as rock.

"Bill?" Lizzy shouted. "Is that you?"

He didn't want to reach the shore. The thought of cooking dinner and making stilted conversation before avoiding sex—it was unbearable. But the only words left to say— *I don't love you anymore*—were not in Bill's vocabulary. He stopped paddling and looked into the almond-colored water, understanding that Renée's death had not been a mistake.

"Bill?" called Lizzy.

He stood up in the boat, while she could still see him, and took off his shirt. The evening air was chilly, bringing goose bumps to his skin. He sat down, took off his sneakers and his socks.

"Bill!" She had abandoned her magazine, and was running to the edge of the deck. He rose again, and unclasped his buckle, removing his jeans and underwear. He faced his wife, and then he dove into the lake. The cold was a shock, but he swam down, trying to touch the bottom. For a moment, he was still, and then he floated up, breaking out of the water and taking a deep breath. "Come swimming!" he shouted.

There was no answer.

A last time, he said, "Come swimming!" And then he waited, treading cold water. A cloud moved across the moon.

Bill tried to find a star, to make a wish, but the sky was a uniform dark blue. The water stung his eyes, and he closed them. There was a splashing sound—the sound of waves, or maybe the smooth strokes of someone swimming toward him. In the twilight, one loon sang out. The cry was beautiful and lonely.

# Shakespeare.com

Raul was talking to me about the *Hamlet* product. The bathroom was full, the parking lot under the ramp to the Bay Bridge was full, every damn cubicle was occupied. I was drinking tea like it was going out of style. In the kitchen area there were two giant coffeemakers, an espresso machine that no one knew how to use, and some chocolate-covered coffee beans. Shakespeare.com was all about caffeine, and yet I sipped decaf, as Dr. Zhong had ordered.

Raul was using words like *focus group* and *unit sales*. We were Editorial. We should have been using words like *semicolon* but here we were, on the verge of our next round of funding, everything strained to the breaking point (we had switched to Airborne Express when FedEx had cut us off, then to bike messenger, and finally back to FedEx but using our own personal credit cards), and even in Editorial we were talking about Sales.

My period was ten days late, and I was beginning to get excited.

The artists were upstairs. They were mashed in like sardines and wore cat-eye glasses and faux-fur coats, most of them stoned most of the time. I had to tell Jesus that his drawing of Curious George dressed like King Lear was not going to fly.

"But it's Curious George," he said, sliding his earphones from his ears. "Kids like Curious George."

"I'm not trying to be difficult," I said, "but what does a monkey have to do with the theme of the play? Not to mention copyright issues . . ."

Jesus stared at me levelly. I touched my hair.

"Dude," said the woman next to Jesus, "what about a giant fucking milk shake, with, like, a talking straw? 'I'm King Lear, I'm King Lear!' "

Jesus and the woman cracked up. "You got it," said Jesus. "You fucking said it." He laughed until tears leaked from the corners of his eyes.

"Hmmm," I said. "Well, get back to me on that." I saw a temp in a halter top leave the bathroom door open and I ran for it.

Between my legs, a white expanse of cotton. I closed my eyes and breathed out, then stood and washed my hands with the Softsoap on the counter. There was a *Hustler* magazine next to the toilet, and a half-empty bottle of red wine. The bathroom window was open—I could hear the yelling. Next door to our office (which used to be a tai chi studio) was a garage. Outside the garage, men yelled at each other in Russian. Periodically, they discarded scraps of metal on the sidewalk—car doors, hubcaps. Once a month or so, a brand-new car for sale appeared outside the shop. The garage was a front for something, but we weren't sure what.

I dried my hands and saw Ben the Tech Guy walking up to our office door leading a puppy on a piece of string. By the time I got downstairs to my cubicle, Ben the Tech Guy was wandering around, telling everyone he had found the puppy at the bus stop and could it live in someone's cube for a while? It could eat pretzels, he insisted.

We had the Monday Editorial Meeting at ten. All of us rose from our cubicles and tramped purposefully up the stairs: Betty, in a flowered dress; Raul and Edward, who had just fallen in love and begun to wear each other's clothing; Linda the yoga queen; and Joni the *Othello* expert, in a see-through leopard-print dress from Express.

When we opened the door, strange faces stared at us: adults, real adults, in suits. The meeting room was full of the venture capitalists who wrote our paychecks. I whispered, "*We're* supposed to have ten o'clock!" and Brendan grabbed my arm from behind. Brendan was the founder of Shakespeare.com. He was also the CEO, CFO, and Editor-in-Chief. He wore corduroy pants and used hair gel.

"Carry on," Brendan said to the adults, who looked mildly uncomfortable in our meeting room, which we had painted neon green. Brendan closed the door. "Let's meet in the alternate area," he said.

The alternate area was Sombrero's, the Mexican restaurant across the street. We sat around a Formica table shaped like a jalapeño. Betty sat next to me. She smelled of baby powder. "Are you sick?" she asked me, tucking into her breakfast—three tacos, refried beans, and a large Coke.

"What?" I said. "Do I look sick?"

"You're pale," said Raul.

"And your hair is flat," said Edward. They laughed cattily.

Brendan called the meeting to order. "Let's start with the new marketing campaign," he said. He drew envelopes on his place mat with a ballpoint pen. Then, he drew a row of circles. Lastly, another row of envelopes. "We have a three-pronged attack," he said.

I said, "This is the Monday Editorial Meeting."

"Oh," said Brendan. He sipped his Mr. Pibb. "Does anyone have any Editorial issues?"

There was silence. I tried to decide if I should give voice to my concerns about the King Lear monkey/milk shake concept. Betty cleared her throat and asked, "Any news on funding?" I noticed that her hand was in a fist in her lap.

"Very soon," said Brendan. "Very soon there should be some news."

"Payday is Thursday," said Edward. "Are we going to

get paid?" Raul put his hand on Edward's shoulder and squeezed.

Brendan cleared his throat. "Why don't I fill you in on the new marketing campaign?" he said expectantly. We nodded.

He went on and on. Basically, the new marketing campaign was to mail a bunch of stuff. My head was pounding from lack of caffeine. Everyone around me slurped happily, and with verve. Their eyes lit up as the wondrous drug hit their nervous systems. They began making comments about the new strategy, seasoned comments about target customers and data spreads. Linda the yoga queen stretched her arms toward the fluorescent light on the ceiling: Sitting Mountain Pose.

Shakespeare.com had a chance. We'd gone through two rounds of funding already, and we were waiting for our third. The first six months had been heady: Free Barbecue Wednesdays, Beer Fridays, and pizza everywhere. We had a snack shelf then, filled with Gummi Bears and granola bars. There had been a soda machine with the coin part turned off: just punch a soda and there you go. Sprite? Sure! Diet Coke? Why not? I had gotten up to seven sodas a day.

By the second round, we were more careful. The office had begun to fill up with employees, and we stopped getting kegs for everybody's birthdays. People started going into the bathroom to do drugs. No more X in the office place. We had investors checking up on us now, parking their Benzes in front of the office, "stopping by." (One investor's license plate said "4TH IPO.") We got benefits and our first employee over thirty—a platinum blond human resources director who wore denim miniskirts. At the last birthday party, which was mine, Brendan bought a cake from Costco and offered everyone ice water. We knew then that we were in trouble.

Let's be frank. Shakespeare.com had started as a good idea: bring Shakespeare to the masses. But it was headed nowhere fast: Shakespeare for idiots. We were actually talking to the "For Idiots" franchise about a possible crossover deal.

I had five hundred thousand stock options. My car was an '83 Civic, my house in Bernal Heights had termites, we slept on a mattress on the floor, and we drank whatever beer was on sale. My husband, Leo, taught first grade. Most weekends, we'd load up the car with camping gear and take Moxie, our lab, to Tahoe or the Santa Cruz mountains. As I made noodles on the camp stove and Moxie ran around in circles, Leo read me *New Yorker* short stories or articles from the *Bay Guardian*. After dinner, we played cards with headlamps on, and I usually—but not always—won.

Leo called these days the Golden Age. "This is the Golden Age," he'd say, head resting on his tanned arms. He would usually begin this train of thought when I mentioned expensive sushi lunches, someone's brand-new VW Bug with the flower holder, or my desire for a shoe shopping spree. "Everybody's feeling flush, starting to forget that times like these don't go on forever." He'd turn to me and smile. "Gotta enjoy the hell out of these days," he would say, "because they won't last." I knew he was thinking of the dinosaurs, his students' favorite subject. The dinosaurs hadn't known what was about to hit them. (My husband believed it was an asteroid.)

We had been trying to get pregnant for some time. San Francisco had sun. It had the ocean. It had parks through which we could push a stroller, holding hands or holding lattes. That was enough. We were ready.

Some people in our office had kids. Jesus had a little boy named Kenneth Hendrix. Jesus said his son could use Kenneth for now, Hendrix for when he was ready to get chicks. Ben the Tech Guy had a daughter named Rocket.

Some people were pregnant. There was Trudy the Temp, whose Italian-American husband wouldn't let her eat salt or drive anywhere herself lest she harm Antonio (or Antonia) Junior. And there was Glenda, who hadn't known she was pregnant until she was five months along. In fact, I had been drinking vodka cranberries with her the night before she went to the doctor. She thought she was just getting fat.

Glenda could eat salt. In fact, she and her husband, a roasting technician at Starbucks, thought that smoking pot in moderation could actually help things in the uterine area.

After the first year or so of gleeful fucking had not resulted in a baby, my husband and I started to get serious. We got poked and prodded and tested, but the doctor said there were no problems. It was something magic, I guess, and it wasn't working for us. Each month I got my period, and it had started to make me teary.

Everyone at Shakespeare.com had opinions. They had opinions on music (pro–Santana), opinions on food (pro-tofu), opinions on what was cool and what was not. In essence, whatever sucked was something you could be proud of liking, because you were saying that you knew it was lame-o and you thought that was funny. You could like Hello Kitty, and you could like gas station hot dogs, but talking about liking your husband was queer. (Having a husband was sort of queer. It was better to be queer.) Real emotion was out. Roller skates were in. Bowling was in, as well.

Linda the yoga queen had told me about Dr. Zhong. Everyone in her Ashtanga class started going to him when they couldn't get pregnant because they didn't have enough body fat. He was an acupuncturist, and the story was, it worked.

I went to Dr. Zhong. His office was feng-shuied out. It was on Clement, and when you walked in, some gong job sounded. There were plants situated in various corners, and a fish tank by the door, which was to invite the money chi inside. A woman with an unstable look in her eyes took my name and told me to sit on a red pillow in the corner. I was not sure if I was in the love corner or the success corner. Either way.

One of the guys on the *Hamlet* team at work told me that Dr. Zhong had changed his life. He had unblocked his entire stomach with Dr. Zhong. Well, not his stomach, he said, but the stomach energy flow. Energy was called *Qi* in acupuncture, he told me earnestly. Whatever: I wanted a baby.

I had always imagined a little boy. Not that I would have minded a daughter, but I relished the thought of a boy who would go with me to the library, who wouldn't mind the stink of the sea lions on Pier 39—or if he did, that was okay, we could skip it—who would kiss me on the cheek and linger, whispering, "Mama."

And I married the right man. It took me a while to find him, and to understand that kindness was what mattered. A man who made a papier-mâché Abraham Lincoln head to wear the day he taught his students about presidents—that was the man my son would have as a father.

There was Dr. Zhong coming toward me, wearing a white coat like a normal doctor. His face was a big pie, and he didn't seem jerky, or in a hurry, like my HMO guy who had a hundred patients a day. He was almost bald, and there was something on his cheek: a birthmark in the shape of a heart. He smiled, thin but wide.

"I'm Mimi," I said. With difficulty, I stood up from the pillow.

"Come with me," said Dr. Zhong.

I did. He led me into a room with a bed inside it. Another woman was there too, in a white coat like Dr. Zhong's. She smiled and Dr. Zhong said, "Lin does not speak English." I nodded. "Why not lie down?" said Dr. Zhong. Why not indeed? The bed was cool underneath my thighs. "Why not tell me why you are here?" said Dr. Zhong, and I began.

"I want to have a baby," I said. "My husband and I have tried everything. I love him, and the doctors say there isn't any reason why." The woman nodded, and took my wrist. Dr. Zhong took my other wrist. I sat between them for a moment, breathing slowly in and out. The woman spoke in Chinese and Dr. Zhong responded. Finally, he said, "It is like a river, with too much water between the banks."

While I considered that, the woman left. "Lie back down," said Dr. Zhong. "Just relax. We will warm your womb."

I really do think he said that. I would not make this up. He stuck needles in various parts of me and then the woman came back with a heat lamp and held it in front of my belly button. They took some big rubber cups and suctioned them on and off of me. And then it was done. "Take this," said Dr. Zhong, handing me a piece of paper covered in Chinese characters.

I took the pills and sipped the tea. The tea tasted like what would result if you boiled lemongrass and Windex. Fucking A. I drank the stuff. When I told my husband all about it, he laughed and then looked a bit miserable. He patted the spot next to him on the mattress, and I went and lay down. He ran his fingers through my hair. "Hey," he said. There was nothing else to say. He wanted a little one as much as I did.

I felt a bit different after Dr. Zhong. I slept more soundly than ever before. It was as if my life had stopped while I was asleep—none of those half-remembered turnings, no dog jumping on the bed and mashing my feet. It was as if I had been alone in bed and taken NyQuil. NyQuil rocked. It had been like that. And then I woke up.

I should have gotten my period on Thursday. Thursday came and went, and I ran into the bathroom whenever it was free, which was not often. My heart raced as I copyedited the synopsis of *Othello*. (Each play was synopsized into short, "reader-friendly" segments. For example, here is what I was handed on Thursday: *Othello was a totally rad dude and he told crazy stories. He was black; which is totally cool; but which was not cool in Shakespeareses time. Desdemona was a young hottie, like Christina Aguilera, but royalty. She fell in love with Othello. They were like Iman and David Bowie; but opposite.* Unbearably, it was not my job to rewrite the "story pods," as they were called. I just added apostrophes, deleted semicolons, gritted my teeth, and moved on.)

As I made pancakes on Sunday, my husband said, "Shouldn't you have gotten your period by now?" He was reading the "Week in Review" section of *The New York Times*.

I looked at the griddle. "Don't say anything else," I said. I flipped a pancake. Leo pressed his lips together, but could not stop the edges of his mouth from grinning. I ate so many pancakes, thinking that I was eating for two. Thinking that my little boy would love my pancakes, the way I mix butter and syrup together in a pan.

. . .

After the Monday Editorial Meeting, I went for a walk. I needed exercise, not caffeine. Shakespeare.com was in a dangerous part of town. We had no sign on our door, and an amazing alarm system to protect all the iMacs the artists used.

The street we were on, Bryant, was a busy street in disrepair. It was foggy as hell, and I shuffled along, past all the Mexican restaurants and the body shops. I passed Karry's Collision Center and the Chair Place. A teenage girl with bags of groceries got off a bus, followed by two little boys wearing baseball caps. The girl yelled at her sons in Spanish, and they each took a bag from her. In the doorway of a liquor store, a man with a sunburn drank from a paper cup. The marquee above Jovita's Restaurante y Cantina read: POINTY BONE TUES.

At the corner of Second and Bryant was Margarita the Psychic. I guess I had been walking toward her all along. A sandwich board on the sidewalk featured a giant hand and a picture of Margarita (a buxom babe with flowers in her hair). The building was green, and heavy curtains covered the windows. I walked over the cracked pathway. My face was damp, and I could smell my BO rising from my armpits. I had begun to sweat a Windexy smell since drinking Dr. Zhong's tea.

I could hear *Montel* on the television from behind the door. I knocked, and a little girl's voice said something in Spanish. I had to learn Spanish! Just thinking of the lives I was missing, the rivers of conversation around me, all that I was excluded from due to my inability to sit down with some damn vocabulary book—well, it made me want to cry.

The door opened. In front of me stood an old woman, very old. I mean, she was leaning on a walker. "Eh?" she said.

"Is Margarita here?" I said. This lady looked nothing like the sign.

"Margarita inside, Margarita inside," said the old lady. Despite the heat, she wore a blue electric blanket over her shoulders, the cord trailing, unplugged, behind her. Her hair was matted on one side, and she did not appear to have teeth.

"I think I'll come back another time," I said. I nodded, trying to be encouraging, trying to ignore the sour fear that had shot from my feet to my scalp.

The woman grabbed my hand. Her fingers were dry and cold. I pulled away. There was a smell of something burning. "Inside, inside," said the old lady, reaching for me again. I felt weak. I wanted to leave, but did not know what to say, what neurons to fire to move my limbs in such a way that would result in me sitting at home, in my husband's lap, hearing him say, "Hey."

The lady got a grip on my arm. She pulled me in.

The front room was filled with shitty furniture and a million cats. The place smelled like urine. Good God. The woman shoved me into a Barcalounger. "Here, here," she said, and she held her hands flat in front of her, as if to push me down if I tried to rise.

"I've got to get back to work," I said.

"No, no," she said. "No, no." She seemed alarmed, and although my adrenaline rush had ebbed to a nice fatigue in my arms, a nugget of nausea remained. The woman disappeared into a back room, and I could hear her speaking rapidly. I looked around at the velvet paintings on the wall, the batch of Virgin Mary candles on the mantel. *Montel* had been switched off, but a cup of juice and a half-eaten bag of pork rinds remained on the floor.

The old woman shuffled back into the room. "Margarita, Margarita!" she said, her eyes shining with excitement, her face flushed. I could have used a margarita, alrighty. The lady lifted a bony arm and extended a finger toward the door.

It opened, and with a flourish, a middle-aged woman with a turban on her head walked in. "I am Margarita," she said. "Welcome, my dear." The turban was fashioned from a towel; I could see San Francisco Giants insignias on it. Margarita wore a green T-shirt and Jordache jeans.

"Uh," I said.

Margarita sat on the floor in front of my Barcalounger, crossing her legs Indian style. Her feet were bare, and her toenails were painted a light pink. "How are you?" said Margarita.

"I'm fine," I said.

"Ah," said Margarita, deciding to pick up the pace. "I see a man, a man for you." I sighed. She pinched her eyelids shut and began to nod. "Oh," she said. "Oh, now I can see it." The old lady nodded approvingly, reaching for the pork rinds.

"What?" I said.

"You and this man," she said. "You and this tall man. You will fall in love."

In spite of myself, I became intrigued. Leo *was* tall, after all. Margarita was moving her arms around in front of her, making humming noises. Her T-shirt was tight across her chest; she wore no bra. She writhed around as if in rapture. Finally, she pressed her fingers to her eyes. After a moment, she dropped her hands to her lap and looked at me.

"Well?" I said.

"I see red," she said. "Red, the color of roses."

Hmmm. Well, if I press my eyelids, I see red too, but I took two fives from my pocket and gave them to her. She and the old lady bid me farewell and switched that TV right back on before I was even down the walkway. I could hear Montel pontificating all the way down the block.

On the way back to the office, I stopped at the Happy Mexican Gas Mart. There was a man talking on a cell phone behind the counter. Next to him, a thuggy teen ate a Dove bar, the ice cream melting down his wrist. Periodically, the man on the cell phone grabbed the Dove bar and took a bite.

I wandered the aisles of the Happy Mexican, looking for a pregnancy test. I thought about how I would tell my husband the news. I could take him out to dinner, and call for a toast to our baby. I could buy some cheesy Hallmark card, or hang a banner in our doorway. I could buy a tiny pair of shoes and wrap them up. Tiny sneakers? Tiny moccasins?

I decided that I would bring Dr. Zhong some flowers. Daisies, maybe, or lucky palm stalks. I would walk right past that unstable woman and her jars, and Dr. Zhong would light up at the sight of me, the mother-to-be.

I bought the test and a Snickers in the Happy Mexican. I ate the candy bar on the way back to the office, and the chocolate on my teeth was hot and wonderful. My headache almost went away. I decided to tell my husband in bed. I would pull the covers over our heads and whisper the news. He would hug me, and I would hear his breath become ragged.

Back in the office, the stray dog was chewing on my computer cord. It was a little black thing, with a tail that curled around like a pig. I took it into my arms, and it was just the right weight, and warm.

When an anorexic artist left the bathroom, I went inside. I opened the cardboard box and tried not to look at the blond woman smiling ear to ear on its cover, holding up her pregnancy test with a big plus sign, her wedding band flashing. I looked at my own wedding band—a silver one we had bought in Mexico. The directions seemed simple: pee on the stick, and wait.

The Russian men next door were yelling, and I unbuttoned my jeans. I closed my eyes and prayed, to what I don't know, to something. To Dr. Zhong. To Margarita. I unwrapped the plastic stick. But before I could begin, I looked down.

Just as Margarita had foreseen, my underwear was red as roses. I think I cried out, but there was no one there to listen. Everyone at Shakespeare.com had gathered in the conference room for the big announcement. When I came out of the bathroom, Betty told me the news. Seven million dollars of funding had come through, and Brendan had bought fifty boxes of Girl Scout cookies to celebrate. I ate Thin Mints for a while, and then I ate Tagalongs.

When I told Leo, over dinner, that I was only eating for one, he looked down quickly at the napkin in his lap. His eyelashes were long and dark—they shielded his eyes from me.

On Monday, Brendan sent an e-mail saying, "Dear Mimi, Please stop by my office at your convenience. Yours truly, Brendan." I stood and walked the ten feet to where he sat behind a big IKEA desk. Brendan made a pyramid of his fingertips. "Don't take this wrong," he said, "but I've heard about your troubles." I blinked. "My sister adopted," he continued, "a little baby from Romania. A boy, Jack." Brendan looked at me pointedly.

"Word travels fast," I said.

"Well," he said, "it is a small office. Anyway, I told her about you, and she'd be happy to meet you for lunch, if you're interested." He wrote a phone number on an envelope and pushed it across his desk. He stood. "Well, then," he said, smoothing his Dockers.

I took the number. "I thought you were going to fire me," I said.

Brendan laughed, but not in a very reassuring manner.


"Look at him," said Brendan's sister. We were sitting in Sombrero's and there was a baby on the table, between our empanadas. It was a beautiful baby, with brown wisps of hair and fat cheeks.

"You'd never even know he was Romanian," said Brendan's sister, a very thin woman with lipstick the color of cherry tomatoes. Jack, in his baby seat, slept peacefully, despite the jangling Mexican music. "I don't see the need to tell anyone he's Romanian," said Brendan's sister.

"What?" I said.

"He looks just like an American boy. He looks like he could be mine. Well, he is mine, isn't he!" she said. Brendan's sister gave me a videotape with a label that read *Weensy Miracles* in pink script. "You can pick a baby from the video," said Brendan's sister.

"It's so easy," I said.

"That's what I'm saying," she said. She told me not to be upset by the babies in the tape who swayed back and forth. "If nobody rocks a baby, they rock themselves," she explained.

That night, my husband and I opened a bottle of wine. We slipped underneath our cotton comforter, resting bowls of pasta on our laps, and when the light in the bedroom was silver, we put the tape in the VCR. Between us, there was a warm space for a baby.

On the television, a man with gray hair and a long mustache walked around a dim room packed with children. From giant, slatted cribs, he picked up infants. For the camera, he held the babies aloft, turning them around, so that people like me could see they were unblemished. He did not stop for the larger children, and just as Brendan's sister had warned, they lined up in rows, their fingers wrapped around the crib slats, rocking themselves back and forth. The tape went on, the man picking up baby after baby.

I watched the faces of the children who were not chosen by the man. When he came near them, some reached up, but did not look surprised when they were passed over. They stared with a dull hatred at the camera, as if they could see into my bedroom: blue coverlet, leafy trees outside large windows, warm bowls of linguine, a bottle of wine on a hardwood floor.

When I looked at my husband, he was completely still, watching the video intently. I turned back to the screen, and I wondered if the dinosaurs had felt anything as the asteroid headed toward them, if they had known it was coming.

## The Way the Sky Changed

I had heard about the rib, of course, but did not expect it to be at the Smiths' Christmas party. Yet there it was, on the mantel, sandwiched between a bowl of cinnamon-scented potpourri and a holly sprig. Merry Christmas! Here's our daughter's rib.

There were pictures of her all over the house. Maybe they had always been there, I don't know. But the one of me and Helen, before our senior prom—it was too much. I stood in the kitchen and drank Scotch fast. My husband would have told me to take it easy, pardner, but he was gone too, and not even a rib to show for himself. My mother came into the kitchen and took in the scene: me, a ham sandwich, an empty glass.

"How are you?" she said.

"The ham is delicious," I noted.

"From Harrington's in Greenwich," she said.

"Really?"

"Same as last year," said my mother. I nodded. "Same as the year before that," she said.

"Is that right?" I said.

"Yes," said my mother.

In the dining room, I found my sister, Jennifer. She was pregnant and miserable. She wore a Burberry headband and her roots were showing. "I've never been sober at one of these before," she said. "It's hell."

I laughed. "You might have a husband, but at least I can drink," I said. Jennifer turned those brown eyes on me.

"Why do you go and say things like that?" she said. I shrugged. "Did you call my therapist?" she said. "I'm going to keep asking, Casey, till you make an appointment."

"I made an appointment," I said. "I'm going next Thursday."

"Really?" said Jennifer.

"Yes, really," I said. "What am I, a four-year-old?"

"I'm glad," said Jennifer, touching my arm. "Alexa has really helped me with my panic disorder. Alexa and the Zoloft."

"I wonder why a rib," I mused.

Jennifer sighed. "What?"

"It's just so . . . random. Why a rib? Why not a collarbone?" Jennifer looked intently at the wallpaper behind me, a
mélange of African animals. "How are you feeling?" I asked.

"What?"

"I mean with the morning sickness and all. Do you feel
crummy?"

"Yes," said Jennifer.

"Me too," I said. "But I'm not pregnant."

"No," said Jennifer. "You're not."

We had thought about it, Paul and I. There had always
been a reason to believe the next year would be a better year
to become parents. Paul's bonus, my big new writer. Fucking
Hal Underson, whose novel, *A Kiss in Kandahar,* finally went
to a lousy little press in St. Louis. I'd had big plans for Hal,
maybe even a movie deal. My 15 percent of Hal was about a
thousand dollars. So we'd waited.

"No," I said to my sister. "I'm not."

Jennifer's husband, Lawrence, came up behind her, holding out a mini quiche. "Yummy," he said, pushing the morsel
toward Jennifer's mouth.

"Get it away from me," said Jennifer.

"Suit yourself," said Lawrence.

"Suit yourself?" I said. "Are we really old enough to say
'Suit yourself'?" I laughed, but then realized that both Jennifer and Lawrence were sober.

"Casey," said Jennifer, "Lawrence has a friend you should
meet. He's in arbitrage, a really nice guy. Skidmore BA, Har-
vard MBA."

"Jen," said Lawrence, "perhaps this isn't the best of times?"

"Are you quoting Dickens?" said Jennifer.

"I'm trying to be thoughtful," said Lawrence.

"What's this guy's name?" I interrupted.

"Kent," said my sister.

"Oh," I said. "Kent? Are you sure?"

"He is nice," admitted Lawrence.

"Nice dull?" I said.

"No, nice like he's not an asshole," said Jennifer.

"Is he my type?" I said.

Jennifer and Lawrence looked uncomfortable. "I have a type," I said. "And it's tall and blond. Ponytailed, actually."

Lawrence cleared his throat. "But Paul is . . . I mean Paul was . . ."

"Just because I married a short Jew doesn't mean I can't have a different type," I said. I laughed, but it came out strangled. "I'm not crying," I explained, "I'm just very tired."

"I'll give him your number," said Jennifer. "Kent."

"Well, I'm off to the bar," I said. I left my sister feeling sorry for me and worried about me. She had enough to worry about, and I wished she'd just ignore me, just treat me like a rib in the corner of the room.


My mother gave me a ride after the party. She asked if I'd like to stay over at home. "I have a home," I said.

"I meant my home," she said.

"Spend the night in my old room, like I'm fifteen?" I said. "No spank you."

"You should really watch it with the booze," said my mother. She put on her blinker and we took a left, out of Indian Village. Underneath the train tracks, some rich kids dressed as poor kids were skateboarding. "Watch it, yo!" yelled a redhead with his pants so low his boxer shorts were showing.

"You know something?" said my mother.

"No," I said. "I don't know anything."

"Well, I'll tell you," said my mother. "You were difficult until the day Paul found you, and then you sweetened for a while. I thought you had changed. But it was just Paul, all along."

I closed my eyes, and things seemed spinny. When I forced them open, my mother was watching me. "It's been over a year," she said. "Now it's up to you to save yourself."

I nodded. "I hear you," I said, and then I threw up.

I had nightmares about Paul's bones coming to find me. I didn't want them, though I had brought his green plastic hairbrush to the police station in a fit of sentimentality. The word around town was that once they matched the DNA, the police would knock on your door with the news. In my town, that fall, we waited.

I guess I hadn't really believed that Helen was gone until the rib arrived. Helen, who had walked hand in hand with me to kindergarten, her brown hair swinging, who had taught me to kiss, pressing her own dry lips to mine. Helen!

Kent called the following week. My assistant, Cindy,

came into my office. "Kent Hornbeck on Line Two," she said.

"Take a message," I said.

She shrugged pertly. Cindy. This gal was all about pert. She came back not a minute later. "He says he's made reservations at Caroline's Comedy Club for Thursday," said Cindy.

"Yuck," I said.

"It's fun," said Cindy.

"You've been to Caroline's Comedy Club?"

"This guy I dated? Thomas Drury? He was big into comedy. It's fun, really."

"Give me that number," I said. I called Kent in arbitrage. I'll be honest: I don't know what arbitrage is. Paul was a lawyer and I'm in publishing. Arbitrage has just never factored in.

Kent answered the phone. I explained that I would not be able to go to Caroline's Comedy Club. "Lawrence told me this might be difficult," said Kent.

"Excuse me?"

"Listen, I've already bought the tickets. It's just a comedy show. I'll meet you there at seven?"

"Fine," I said.

But first there was Alexa, the therapist. She told me to let go of regrets. I told her my mother said I had never been a very nice person. She told me to let go of fear. I told her about the comedy club, and she thought it was a good idea.

Caroline's was crowded and smoky. Kent held my arm as

we wound our way to our seats. One table leg must have been shorter than the rest; the table kept tipping all around. I was tired before our drinks arrived. "So what did your husband do?" asked Kent. I thought this was a strange way to begin a date.

"Lawyer," I said.

"My wife sold software," said Kent.

"Your wife?" I said.

"Wendy," said Kent. "She was on Flight 11."

"I didn't know," I said. What did I want with some widower, I thought. "Jesus, I'm sorry," I said. The waitress returned with our order. She was a bit sour, but I guess you don't have to be funny to serve the drinks.

"Where was he?" asked Kent. "Your husband?"

"The North Tower," I said.

His eyes were dull. "Wendy was in business class," he said. I nodded. "Did he . . . did you talk to him?" asked Kent.

"No," I said. He nodded, and drank his martini quickly. We ordered another round.

The first comedian had bad skin. He told a bunch of jokes about his mother, and then a bunch of jokes about how dumb Cajuns are. I had never met a Cajun, so these jokes were wasted on me. It seemed that Cajuns ate catfish sandwiches and kept alligators as pets. We sipped our drinks sadly, and after the first comedian had finished, I told Kent I was exhausted, went outside, and hailed a cab.

Paul and I used to watch the news after work. One night, a reporter in a blue windbreaker stood in a Kansas parking lot, where a plane had just crashed. "If you were on a plane going down," I said to my husband, "I would not want you to call me. I would rather remember all the good times. Not one last crummy phone call, you know?"

"I don't know," said Paul. "I might want you to call me."

"Well, don't call me," I said. "I'm not interested." In my memory, I say the words so blithely—*I'm not interested*. I was a different person, then.

I think about Paul, trapped in the searing building. I did try his cell phone, but there was no answer. I know that he wanted to dial my number, to say good-bye. I know he didn't jump. Well, I don't officially know, but that's what I think. Maybe he fainted. Maybe it wasn't as bad as I am pretty sure it was. I wish he had called me. I wish I could say to him, *I'm sorry*. I wish he had taken a sick day. But his car was parked at the station when I finally got home from the city. There was his coffee mug. There was his napkin from his English muffin, marked with a butter stain.

Kent called me at work the next morning. "I thought the comedy club would be a good idea," he said, "but I guess maybe it wasn't."

"It was fine," I said.

"I'd like to see you again," said Kent. This surprised me.

"How about cheeseburgers?" I said.

"How *about* cheeseburgers?" said Kent.

He took the train out, and we went to the Rye Grille and Bar. "I've never been to Rye," said Kent. "Scarsdale, yes, but not Rye."

"It's a nice place," I said, though I had begun to wonder if it was the place for me, single and suburbs being a grim combination. When Jan came to take our order, she looked surprised to see me with a date, then angry, then sad.

"What do you recommend?" Kent asked Jan.

"Oh, get a cheeseburger," I said. Paul and I always ordered cheeseburgers.

"The tuna steak sandwich is good," said Jan. She looked Kent up and down. He was cute in a preppy way: the tousled hair, ruddy skin. If you watched him, you could see how he'd looked at five, chasing after frogs or tadpoles with a little net.

"The cheeseburgers are really the best," I insisted.

"I think I'll try the tuna steak sandwich," said Kent. He looked at me with a smile, but he must have seen something in my face. He blinked, and I looked down at my menu. "Wait," said Kent, reaching out and touching his fingers to Jan's arm. "I've changed my mind."

She wheeled around and raised an eyebrow.

"I'll have the cheeseburger after all," said Kent.

"You might even want to try the fried onions on top," I said.

"Oh," said Kent, "okay."

The following Saturday, Kent asked me to go antiquing with him in Connecticut. "There's a great diner in Roxbury," he said, "and then we can go for a hike along this lake." I preferred to spend my Saturdays lying on the lawn and staring at the overgrown patch where I had once tended a garden, but I agreed. Kent brought a pair of ladies' hiking boots. They fit me perfectly, and this seemed to make Kent very happy. I wore my own socks, however. We drove up to Connecticut in Kent's Volvo station wagon. He played tapes of Nina Simone and held my hand when he was not shifting the gears. "I packed a picnic lunch," he confided. "Pâté and grapes and even that pinot noir."

"What pinot noir?" I said.

He looked flustered. "Oh, you'll like it," he said. He squeezed my fingers.

The scenery grew beautiful. Barns and cows and men selling peaches. Kent pulled into the parking lot of an antique store called Mason's. He opened my door and took my hand. "Come on," he said, "I have a surprise for you."

I followed Kent into Mason's. It was a dusty old store filled with junk. Lots of nautical-themed stuff, and a bunch of that Fiestaware. Kent hustled me toward the back, and I pretended to be interested in some old cough medicine bottles. There was music in the store, Billie Holiday. I liked that.

It wasn't long before Kent came back. "It's all arranged," he said, his eyes shining. He took my hand, and led me into a back room. Once there, he gestured to a huge mirror. It was surrounded by an ornate frame. It was unwieldy and ugly.

"Sweetheart," said Kent, "it's yours."

"The mirror?" I said.

He nodded, tears in his hazel eyes.

"Oh, Kent," I said, "it's just what I've always wanted."

"I know," said Kent. He took me in his arms, and whispered, "Sweetheart, I know." After this exchange, we went to a lakeside spot and ate the pâté and drank the pinot noir. Kent did not kiss me.

My mother came over the next day. "What on earth is that?" she said, pointing to the mirror, which was propped up in the front hallway.

"A mirror," I said. "Kent gave it to me."

"My God," she said. "It's hideous."

"Well, okay," I said.

"What are you making?"

"Beef Stroganoff."

"Oh sweetie," said my mother. I stirred the pot, and added salt.

"Would you like some pinot noir?" I asked my mother.

"I only drink pinot grigio and you know it."

"People can change," I said.

"Did you hear about the femur?" said my mother.

"Oh God," I said. I closed my eyes. "You know what?" I said. "I don't want to hear about any femur."

"This isn't any femur, Casey," said my mother. "It's Doug Greenberg's femur."

"Jesus Christ," I said. I had once given Doug a blow job in the back of his father's Porsche.

My mother shook her head. "Tragic," she said, "just tragic. But they're burying theirs, not putting it on the mantel."

I kept stirring. "That smell," said my mother. "That smell makes me think of your father."

"Really?"

"He used to love beef Stroganoff. Don't you remember? He'd call from the station and say, 'Is dinner ready?' and I'd say, 'Yes, dear,' and I'd pack you and your sister in the Oldsmobile and we'd go get your daddy. I'd put you to bed while he had his cocktails and watched the news, and then we'd eat together." The light coming in the kitchen window made my mother's face glow. "That was a good time," she said.

"I used to make it for Paul," I said. "I never knew why."

She smiled at me. "This is just a bad time, honey," she said. "But then it will be a good time again."

"What if it's just going to get worse?" I said.

She looked down at her Gucci pumps. She opened her hands and then pulled them into fists.

That night, after eating three helpings of my beef Stroganoff, Kent asked if he could sleep over, and I said yes. I gave him a pair of Paul's pajamas, and of course Paul's toiletries were all still lined up in the cabinet. Kent was bigger than Paul, so he just wore the pajama shirt and his boxers. He smelled all wrong with the right toothpaste.

My new therapist was not pleased with the news of my budding romance. "What is Kent like?" she asked me.

"He bought me a mirror," I said.

She pursed her lips. "A mirror," said Alexa.

"Yes," I said, "a mirror."

She stared at me for a while, waiting for me to say something more. "It's kind of big," I said.

"Kind of big," said Alexa.

"Yes," I said. "Kind of big and um, dusty. Tarnished."

"Tarnished," said Alexa.

"But I like it," I said. "There's nothing wrong with it. I look in the mirror and I feel better."

"Feeling better does not always mean feeling healthier," said Alexa. I told her I would keep that in mind.

My sister disagreed. "You need love," she told me, as we got pedicures at Nails of America. "We all need love," said Jennifer, and then she began weeping. She was speaking so softly that I had to lean in close to hear her. "It's the hormones," she whispered.

Kent's apartment was cluttered, filled with books. Wendy, it turned out, had been a software salesperson who wanted to be a poet. I was never much for poetry—I liked diving into long, lusty novels—but Kent handed me Robert Frost, and rested his head on my lap while I read.

Some nights, I paged though Microsoft Word printouts on Kent's couch, hoping to find the next Graham Greene, and Kent made elaborate ethnic meals (Indian, Thai, Ethiopian). Wendy had always made the *injera* bread, and I couldn't get the hang of it, so I found a restaurant on Amsterdam and I just picked it up on my way over. Her shoes fit me, which was a bonus, as Wendy had very good taste in shoes. I began jazzing up my outfits with her Fendi heels and Sigerson Morrison slingbacks.

I was there, at Kent's apartment, that Saturday morning. The plan was to have breakfast at Café Con Leche and then head to the Hayden Planetarium, one of Kent's childhood haunts. Kent had once sat through three star shows in a row. He loved the way the sky changed. I was surprised he could still look up.

Wendy had not liked coffee, so I usually brought instant in my purse. I was boiling water when the buzzer rang. I pressed the intercom button. It was the NYPD, said a nice-sounding man. Oh, shit, I thought. What I do not need is Wendy's femur hanging around.

"Kent?" I said. "It's the NYPD."

Kent came out of the bedroom, pulling on a pair of Paul's sweatpants. "Let them in," said Kent quietly.

I am not a stupid woman. I know that Paul was at work on September 11th. He kissed me, caught the train on time. He was at his desk, because he was the sort of man who woke each morning and went where he was supposed to go. Paul was dead. Unless he drove his car to the station, took the train to the plane, and flew to Vegas.

Kent appeared to be having trouble breathing. He bent over and put his hands on his knees, then straightened. He rolled his head to one side and then the other. "Oh God," said Kent, "oh fuck, fuck, fuck." His face was pale: we both knew what was coming. We had two minutes, maybe three, while the cops rode the elevator up and made their way to the apartment door.

"Kent," I said. "Kent, I have something very important to tell you."

"What?" said Kent. "What is it?" Paul's sweatpants were

too short for Kent. Half of his shins showed, and his ankles were not elegant, as Paul's had been.

I felt sick. I took Kent's hand. "If anything happens to you," I said, "I want you to call me. Please, please call me."

"I will," said Kent, "of course I will, I promise."

"I mean it," I said. "I was wrong about Kansas."

I was crying, it seemed. Kent pulled me to him. His heart was hammering against his ribs. I heard footsteps in the hallway, coming toward us. "I'll call you," said Kent. His breaths were short. "I will. But there's something you should know."

There was a knock at the door, a sharp, professional rap. There was shuffling, a clearing of a throat.

"I'll call you, but it won't make any difference," said Kent. "It's all the fucking same, in the end."

He let me go abruptly, and then he unlocked the door and opened it. "Mr. Kent Hornbeck?" said the cop. He was an older man, with lines in his face. His eyes were sympathetic and tired.

"Yes," said Kent.

"May we come in?" said the cop.

Kent looked at me. I closed my eyes. Paul, a Vegas show-girl on his lap. Wendy, writing poetry, snacking on *injera* bread. I opened my eyes, and Kent was looking into them. We both knew it was time to find out what remained.

PART TWO *Lola Stories*

## Miss Montana's Wedding Day

The man Lola loved wasn't marrying her, and she didn't know what to wear to the wedding. For one thing, it was cold in Montana. That ruled out the scorned redhead in a silk dress idea. Also, she would have to wear boots; it had been snowing for weeks. The sun was up, but it was still dark, a gray day. They called it "the inversion," the way wood smoke, soot, and fog hovered over the Missoula valley. You could escape it if you climbed Jumbo or Mount Sentinel—from above, the inversion was a luxuriant cloud.

Lola's windowsill was lined with empty wine bottles. Past the bottles, the tops of the mountains were white with new snow. A darkness filled Lola, and she tried to focus on small, good things. She could eat pizza for breakfast, if she wanted. It was warm in her bed. Chocolate. Her heart was broken, and she honestly felt that way—broken. Her stomach, her head, her arms hurt. It was awful, and worse, it was futile.

What did it say about Lola that she had fallen in love with a man who would leave her for Miss Montana? That she had spent almost a year visiting his cheap Rattlesnake rental, pretending to enjoy baked beans dumped on spaghetti, kissing him even when he forgot (in the throes of academic inspiration) to brush his teeth?

It had happened so fast. Lola went home to New York for Christmas vacation, and when she returned, Iain had already met Miss Montana at a Tuesday night showing of *The Blair Witch Project,* shared a few pitchers of beer with her afterward, and ended up in her bed. "It was as if I was possessed. It was, in a word, inevitable," Iain told Lola, with a pained-but-smug expression.

"True love, I guess," Lola said, starting to cry.

Iain said nothing, but nodded. A wedding invitation arrived a few weeks later, with a scribbled note in an unfamiliar hand: *We sincerely hope you can attend.*

Jeans were out. Lola would look as if she were trying to look as if she didn't care. And all she had for fancy was her Rye High School prom dress in salmon pink. ("Wonderful Tonight"? Not for Lola, who spent the whole evening looking for her date, Josh, eventually located passed out in a janitor's closet.) Every item of clothing made Lola think of Iain: the green teddy he had bought her for St. Patrick's Day, the tight Carhartts he liked her in, the skirts he'd whistle at when he saw her across the quad. What use were they? He was marrying Miss Montana.

Iain. The fine arc of his nose, the ticklish beard, blue eyes almost disconcertingly light. His hands on Lola's hips, his mouth on her mouth. Iain's dissertation in progress was called "Tragedy in Shakespeare's *Othello:* Fate or Fecklessness?" He seemed to relish correcting people about the extra "I" in his name.

Lola brushed her long, red hair. In the mirror above her bureau, she looked tired. She was twenty-one, and knew that she should feel her life beginning to flower. Instead, she felt wilted, a Walgreens bouquet. On the other hand, Miss Montana was blooming with Iain's child. He had told Lola, and then dropped her off at her dorm. "I'll never forget you," he added, before pulling away.

In the spring, Lola would finish her junior year at the University of Montana. She was a communications major, which was ironic, because she spoke primarily to a bartender named Cal and her mother. She was a straight-A student, and had won a student internship at the local paper, the *Missoulian,* covering the crime beat.

When she got the letter from Win Johnson, the Lifestyles Editor and Intern Coordinator, Lola had run to Iain's office on campus, interrupting a conference with a freshman by throwing open Iain's door, holding the letter out with both hands, and shaking it, singing, "I got the in-tern-ship, I got the in-tern-ship . . . ," to the tune of "Happy Birthday."

Lola thought she would never return to her mother's house in New York, but as it turned out, she was not going to spend the summer in blissful cohabitation. She would not be putting her books next to Iain's on the shelves, her mayonnaise alongside his ketchup in the refrigerator. The two-week backcountry trip? The advance tickets for the Barry Lopez reading in August? The early-morning yoga class, the kayak for two, the favorite table at Food for Thought, the champagne saved for their one-year anniversary? All of it was worthless.

In addition, the cop beat was depressing—domestic violence, DUIs, marijuana grow labs. When Lola rushed to the scene of a woman stabbed outside the Desperado Sports Tavern, her new notebook in hand, the cop took one look at her and said, "Are you fucking kidding me? They're letting high school kids cover this shit?"

Lola had packed Iain's things (shirts, books, casserole dish) and mailed them to the house Miss Montana had bought with her winnings. The house was a half-minute walk away, but Lola felt a sense of closure about taping shut a box. She had even sent it first class, telling the man at Mail Boxes Etc. that it was her ex-lover's belongings. The man was Native American, and a long braid hung over his maroon Mail Boxes Etc. smock.

"You could have burned these things," said the man. "He is lucky." The man reminded Lola of Paulson, the dark-haired bartender at Ye Olde Maple Tree Inn, where Lola had gone to find her father on the nights he didn't come home in time for dinner.

"He's a jerk," said Lola. The man looked at her sympathetically. "He's marrying Miss Montana," said Lola. She raised her eyebrows.

"Miss Montana?" said the man who resembled Paulson. "Come around here." He led Lola to the employee bathroom. Above the sink was a poster of Jenni Hansen, Miss Montana, in a red-white-and-blue-spangled bikini waving a lasso. "She signed it for me," said the man. He couldn't take his eyes off Jenni, and her winged-out hair. And there it was, in curlicue script: *TO GEORGE*.

For Iain's wedding, Lola decided on a flowered skirt and an oatmeal-colored sweater. She poured food in a bowl for her cat, Sue, locked her room, and rang for the dorm elevator. After a minute, the door next to the elevator banged open. A guy in a backwards baseball cap and boxer shorts stood in the hall for a moment, smelling of beer. His name was Willy. "Whazzup?" said Willy. The elevator arrived, and Lola stepped inside.

"Oh hey, Lola," said Bea, a vivacious cheerleader for the Grizzlies. In the elevator, next to Bea, was an enormous basket of laundry.

"Hey," said Lola.

"What's shaking?" said Bea.

"You don't want to know," said Lola. She pressed LOBBY, though the button already glowed.

"Sure I do," said Bea.

"Remember my boyfriend?" Lola said. "The tall guy, with the beard and the glasses?"

Bea nodded, examining her fingernails. "The old guy?" she said.

"He's getting married," said Lola. "Not to me," she added.

"I need Lee Press-On Nails," said Bea, holding out her hand. The elevator stopped with a jolt and Bea picked up her basket and exited the sliding doors. "You know who else is getting married today?" said Bea, over her shoulder, "is Miss Montana."

In Pat's Hiway Café, Lola ordered coffee and toast. She was surrounded by men drinking. Pat's was connected to a bar, and patrons passed back and forth between the two. What the hell? Lola ordered a beer.

Her toast dripped with butter. She spread jam over it, chewing slowly. Except for the wedding, she had absolutely nothing to do until Monday, when she would return to work, sitting at a desk that belonged to Michelle Lowry, an Arts reporter on maternity leave. Michelle had left a cable-knit cardigan on the back of the chair, two pictures of her husband (fly-fishing and wearing a cheap tux) on the desk, and three Slim-Fast bars in her drawer.

The snow turned to rain, and Lola considered it blearily. She would have to walk to Iain's wedding, ten blocks or so away. Her coffee was weak, and she was happy when the waitress brought a glass of Alaskan Amber. But even the beer made her think of Iain. He loved beer.

The church was completely full. Lola wedged her way between two girls with cameras, and found a seat next to Juli

Lewis, the martini-drinking piano player from the Holiday
Inn Lounge.

"Oh, honey," Juli said to Lola, patting her knee. Juli wore
a red muumuu.

"Oh, well," said Lola. Television cameras were set up
along the aisle, and people held cardboard signs: WE LOVE
YOU JENNI! MONTANA FOREVER! MARRY ME INSTEAD!

Iain and Lola had attended Easter Mass at this same
church the year before. They were still a bit drunk from the
previous night, and had fought so hard for so long that they
couldn't remember what was wrong anymore. The fight had
started with Lola's assertion that Clinton was a disappointment. Iain agreed, but thought Lola let her emotions get
the best of her—feeling betrayed by a philandering Presi-
dent was absurd, he said. Lola didn't like his tone—it was
condescending—and on it went. While the choir sang like
angels, Iain took Lola's hand, held it tenderly. "We are going
to make it," he had said.

Lola saw Iain's mother and father, whom she recognized
from photographs. In the back of the church, reporters
crouched next to the life-size figure of Mary. Pale shadows
from the stained-glass windows made the chaos into a kalei-
doscope, and in the middle was Iain. He was freshly showered (Lola could not help but think of his wet nipples, the feel
of him, his strong hands on her body) and wore a gray suit.
Lola had never seen him dressed up; he had always worn
frayed shirts and jeans.

There was a hush, and the music began. Lola looked
around the church, trying not to make eye contact with any

of Iain's friends. There was a palpable sense of excitement in the air. Although Jenni could be seen around Missoula a few days a week, at ribbon-cutting ceremonies or auto shows, attending her wedding was something people would talk about for years to come. The paper had been analyzing her dress and profiling honeymoon possibilities (Jenni and Iain had opted for a Caribbean cruise and to hell with Montana, but people still loved her).

"This is ridiculous," Robert, an NYU School of Journalism grad, had complained. Robert later got the front page for his exclusive interview with Jenni, in which she described her "summer fairy" wedding dress.

"On the most important and loving day of my life," said Jenni, in the interview, "I want to look like a summer fairy, to show my beloved that we will have days of summer always. In our hearts, I mean." When Lola read the piece, she laughed, but then felt tears sting at the corners of her eyes. After a few minutes, she sighed and began typing her latest article, "Bonner Meth Lab Busted!"

(At the lab, housed in a trailer, Lola had found a black cat among the methamphetamine ingredients. It purred as soon as she picked it up, and she took it back to her room and named it Sue, short for Sudafed.)

The bridesmaids entered slowly, in powder blue dresses with hoop skirts. They held bouquets of blue-colored carnations. Carnations were Jenni's favorite flower, she had said in the exclusive interview, because they "could be dyed any color of the rainbow."

Iain made his way to the front of the church. His loping gait was the same, and he looked down at the petal-strewn aisle. Lola felt a scream inside her, and as if on cue, trumpets blared. In came Miss Montana.

How she had gotten permission to bring a horse into the church Lola did not know. But there it was: a white steed, its saddle trimmed with carnations. Atop the horse, sidesaddle, was Jenni. Her dress was a marshmallow confection, swirls of taffeta and tulle like a Dairy Queen soft serve. Jenni's skin, in January, was a triumphant orange. Her teeth glowed, and she wore eye shadow the color of antifreeze coolant. A fountain of filmy veil was attached to her curls. In one hand she held a bouquet of multicolored carnations, in the other a lasso. As the band struck up the University of Montana Grizzlies fight song, she spun the lasso high above her head and aimed. The crowd grew silent.

And what do you know, the toast of Montana lassoed herself a man. Lola's man: Iain. Lola put her hands to her face, feeling his shame. Iain, his melancholy voice. His hair falling in front of his eyes as he graded papers. She remembered the night they had stayed up until dawn, reading *Antony and Cleopatra* aloud, making funny voices for all the characters but growing serious during the dramatic scenes. She turned to look at him, her love.

In a lasso of gold, he was beaming. His chin was lifted high, and his eyes, usually heavy-lidded, were wide open. He looked at Jenni with all the joy Lola had never thought was in him.

· · ·

Cal shrugged and poured the whiskey. "What?" said Lola.

"Isn't dark yet," said Cal.

"It's dark in here, that's for sure," said Lola. Cal shrugged again. The neon beer signs made his face shine, and he ran a palm over his forehead. On either side of Lola, men with sunken faces drank and stared ahead, at the dusty bottles, at nothing. There was one woman with a glass of white wine. She wore a violet-colored blouse with white buttons. At night, the bar was filled with students playing pool, but for the afternoon crowd, there was only the hum of the heater and the scent of peanuts and wet wool.

"He did it," Lola said. "He tied the knot, all right." Cal nodded. He knew everyone's secrets. In fact, he had probably been there the night that Iain went home with Miss Montana instead of Lola.

"Do you watch people, Cal?"

"What's that?"

"Do you watch people, I said. What they do, how much they drink, et cetera." A man with a large, wet gash in his cheek glanced at Lola sideways, and moved over a stool. The white wine woman looked up.

"What choice do I have?" said Cal.

Lola felt the same way. She didn't think it was right to ignore the sadness around her—alcoholics like her father, lonely women like her mother, who told Lola, "Maybe he would have stayed if I had done my sit-ups. Then again, maybe it was just a mistake from the start."

Lola thought there was something to be proud of in this—in seeing the painful truth—but Iain had jumped on the first cruise ship that passed by, leaving Lola stuck on Misery Island. She had to admit the essential difference between Iain and herself: he believed in the possibility of a carnation-strewn, uncomplicated life, and Lola did not. Perhaps Iain had thought he could convince her, but grew weary of the endeavor.

"I bet you could tell some stories, Cal," said Lola.

Cal took a toothpick from a box underneath the counter and put it in his mouth. "No," he said.

"Can of Bud," said a man on Lola' s left, leaning his elbow on the counter. His cracked leather jacket smelled like sweat. The man had very small feet in pointy boots. Cal cracked the can open with a sharp sound and set it on the counter. The man pulled out some dirty bills, and then twisted the tab back and forth, waiting for his change. He finally broke the tab off and left it on the bar, taking a swig of his can on the way back to his table.

"Come on, Cal," said Lola. "What about love stories?"

Cal sighed, and out of the corner of Lola's eye, she saw the white wine woman reach out. Her lips curled up—a flash of smile, and then it was gone—as she took the beer tab in her fingers, and stuck it behind her bra strap.

"There are no love stories in this town," said Cal.

## Nan and Claude

When her daughter, Lola, called to say she had eloped to Las Vegas, Nan Wilkerson drove straight to her hairdresser's house. Her appointment was not until the following Tuesday, but this was an emergency.

"Nan!" said Claude, opening the door. "What can I do for you?"

"I know it's Saturday," said Nan, "but will you look at these bangs?"

"Hm," said Claude, evaluating. He wore a white button-down shirt, untucked. Claude had his shirts made in his native Paris; the fit was so perfect that he returned each summer for a whole new set.

"I've got a big party tonight at the club," said Nan. "Claude, you've got to help me."

Claude nodded. "Come in," he said.

Years ago, when Nan and Fred had just moved to Rye from the city, Claude had worked at Secrets Salon on Purchase Street. Nan could still remember her first visit to Secrets, the smell of expensive shampoo and ammonia. The salon was filled with young wives Nan wanted to befriend. She had always worn her dark hair in a low ponytail, but that wasn't going to cut it in Westchester.

As Claude had clipped Nan's hair into the style she would wear for the rest of her life, a mid-length bob with bangs, he'd peppered Nan with questions. Where did she live? (The Bruces' old house, on Dogwood Lane.) What did her husband do in the city? (Investment banking.) Golf or beach club? (Golf first—Apawamis, of course—and a beach club later, or even a place for a boat.) How many children did she hope for? (Three, maybe four.) And lastly, whirling her around to face the mirror, what did she think of the *new Nan Wilkerson*?

Nan put her hand over her mouth. It had taken over an hour, but Claude had transformed her into a different person. The sort of person she guessed she was now, a rich man's wife.

"Now get rid of the tennis tan," said Claude, lifting the sleeve of her T-shirt and exposing the pale skin underneath. "Get a bikini, and some brighter lipstick, *cheri*."

Nan was a bit miffed, but knew he meant well. In fact, after buying groceries and gin, she stopped in Village Pharmacy and picked out a slim Revlon tube: Hot Coral.

"Whoa," said Fred, when he arrived home that evening. "Who the hell are you, and what did you do with my wife?"

Nan smiled weakly. "Do you like it?"

"I don't know," said Fred, "and that's the honest truth."

"Well, let me know when you decide," said Nan, in a playful tone.

"Sure will," said Fred, making his way to the bar. "You get more gin?" he asked.

"Yes," said Nan.

"There she is!" said Fred, as Lola, then a wild toddler with strawberry blond curls, came running toward him. But he continued fixing his drink, not bending to pick her up, though she stood with her arms extended, waiting.

It took the Wilkersons two years to get into the Apawamis Club, five more to become Golf Members. Nan worked her way up the Tennis Ladder, and made friends. She became accustomed to days of tennis and poolside lunches, then evenings in the Clubhouse. They moved from Dogwood Lane to a bigger house on Manursing Way. Fred, who had seemed so thrillingly complex and confusing when they were dating—he'd first kissed her in a darkened movie theater during a French film festival, Jacques Demy's *Lola* on the screen—grew fat and angry. He spent weekends drinking wine from a coffee mug and piloting his expensive sit-on-top lawn mower that maybe reminded him of his farm boy past, who knew.

But honestly, what were her options, and dwelling on it certainly didn't help matters. Dancing and cocktailing comforted her during Fred's moods and the three miscarriages.

Fred was on a business trip when she lost the last baby, and he responded to her hysterical call by telling her that his meeting was crucial and he would see her at the end of the week. It was hard on him, too, Nan knew—an unhappy only child, Fred had always wanted a house full of children.

One night, when Lola was twelve, Fred didn't return from the city. Six o'clock came and went. Nan had an appointment with Claude that evening. He had recently left Secrets to start his own salon, Claude's. Getting an appointment was nearly impossible; Nan had been waiting for weeks. "Where the heck is your father?" she said, pacing around the new kitchen, peeking out the sliding glass doors for a glimpse of his BMW. Lola glared steadily at her mother.

"You know, honey," said Nan, "I bet Claude could make your hair a touch less . . ."

"A touch less *what*?" said Lola, her voice dripping with displaced anger. She had been spraying hydrogen peroxide on her hair as she sunbathed, but instead of turning lighter, her hair had become a discomfiting orange. And the neon-colored nets she tied around her head like that singer, Madonna . . . It was hard to know where to start.

"Skip it," said Nan.

"I can stay by myself, Mom," said Lola. "It's not like I'm going to have a keg party or anything."

"Well, and your father should be home any minute," said Nan.

"My *father*," said Lola, and then she made a dismissive *hah*.

Nan picked up her car keys and slipped them in the pocket of her pedal pushers. "I'll be back in two hours," she said. "We can have microwave ribs."

"I'm fine," said Lola.

Nan looked at her for a moment. Clearly, she was not fine. She was confused, lonesome, and about to become a teenager. Nan's heart ached for her. "I love you," said Nan.

"I love you, too," said Lola forlornly, looking up at her mother. Nan went over and hugged Lola, held her close. Their Siamese cat, Bobby, jumped from Lola's lap to the floor. Nan smelled cigarette smoke in her daughter's clothes but said nothing.

"Do you think he's having an *affair*?" said Claude dramatically.

"Right," said Nan, laughing. Claude pressed foil packets full of dye around chunks of her hair. "He's working on a very important deal," said Nan, lying. In truth, as Fred's drinking had grown worse, he'd been cut out of the important deals. Late at night, Nan wondered if her husband would lose his job. Perhaps he had already lost it—he was a mystery to her.

"Of course," said Claude. "He's a very important man, your Fred."

"How is your lovely wife?" said Nan.

"She is wonderful," said Claude.

Nan can still remember returning home that night, eating chewy barbecue while she watched *60 Minutes*. Lola came downstairs as Nan was doing the dishes. "He's left us," said Lola, her eyes puffy from crying.

"What on earth are you talking about?" said Nan.

Lola pointed to their brand-new answering machine. Lola had held her boom box to its speaker the weekend before, painstakingly recording a snippet of song, some druggie woman singing, "If you want me, you can find me left of center, off of the strip." After the song, Lola said flatly, "Please leave your name and number after the beep."

Now, Nan pressed the red button. "Hello, Nan," said Fred's voice. He was carefully enunciating, trying to pretend he was sober. "It's Fred. Look, the time has arrived for me to take a break. This whole lifestyle is killing me . . . the work, work, work, and you—always asking for more, more, more. It's never enough. I just can't do it. So, good-bye, Nan. I'm sorry. Lola, I love you, honey."

Three weeks later, Nan used her daughter's Brother word processor to type up a resume. With shaking hands, she placed it on the desk of the Apawamis Club's personnel director, Kit MacMillan. "Is this a joke?" said Kit, taking off his bifocals to look at Nan.

"It's not a joke," said Nan. "Fred left me."

"Jesus H. Christ," said Kit. But he hired her, and she began lessons right away. On the same court where she'd once reigned supreme, Nan taught her friends' children how to volley and use their backhand. Nan and Lola moved to a small house on the other side of Rye, near the YMCA. Nan's golf caddy lived across the street, and enjoyed fixing cars on his front lawn.

Nan decided that she could not live without Claude, though she could ill afford him. At her next appointment, Claude asked, "So give me the gossip, *cheri*. Was Fred planning a romantic surprise or working late? I want all the details."

Nan contemplated telling the truth for a minute, but when she spoke, her voice was as breezy and sure as ever. "Just as I thought," she said. "A big investment deal. Lucky for him, he did bring roses." At the thought of Fred walking in the front door, holding a box from Rockridge Flowers, Nan's eyes welled up, but Claude was concentrating on her layers, and didn't notice.

"Roses?" said Claude. "So cliché."

"I like roses," said Nan softly. And then it was done: she took a deep breath and complained, as she always had, about the difficulties of managing a house and schisms at the club. As the weeks became months, Nan made up a boyfriend for Lola, fake promotions for Fred, imagined vacations to Venice and St. Barts.

Claude's life also took a turn for the worse: he was spotted inside an AIDS clinic in Port Chester, and as the visible signs of the disease began to appear, he closed Claude's. Whether there had ever been a lovely wife, no one knew for sure. Claude stopped mentioning her, in any case. But Nan continued to visit him twice a month for a cut-and-color at his home, and he pretended to believe she was planning a thirtieth anniversary bash. Maybe he did believe it. Claude's weight dwindled and spots appeared on his skin, but newer drugs kept him alive, and with him, Nan's dreams and her society wife hairdo.

After settling Nan into the salon chair he'd had installed in his guest bathroom, Claude said, "Now tell me about this party at the club."

Nan thought about the photo her daughter had sent from Las Vegas: Lola and a boy drinking champagne, wearing rings. For her wedding, Lola had worn her hair in a ratty ponytail. "Well," said Nan, trying to summon enthusiasm, "it's an engagement party! For Lola, if you can believe it."

"No!" cried Claude. "*Quel surprise!* Tell me everything."

"He's this wealthy boy," said Nan, tipping her head back into Claude's bathroom sink. "Not that it matters, of course. From an oil family in Texas. He wears fancy leather boots with his suits!"

"And where will the wedding be?"

"At Apo, of course," said Nan, though she knew full well the tennis pro was not allowed to have her daughter's wedding at the club, even if Nan had had the twenty grand it would take to pay for the buffet dinner and open bar. Even if Lola hadn't already eloped in the tackiest manner imaginable.

Claude massaged Nan's hair with love. He was the only man who'd touched her in years. He let the warm water run over her scalp, then wrapped her hair in a towel, not the plush ones he'd once had at the salon, but a yellow one, one he likely used himself. She sat up, and regarded herself in his bathroom mirror. Claude put his hands on her shoulders and squeezed. His eyes met hers. The smell of chemicals mixed with the leftover scent of Claude's dinner, most likely from the freezer, probably fish.

"And they'll live happily ever after," said Claude.

# She Almost Wrote Love

After his third marriage went bust, Lola considered finding a wife for her father. He had issues, there was no doubt: he was a terrible father, and unemployed. But there was a certain sweetness in him, despite the cigars and cheese-only diet he had put himself on, his own disgusting take on the Atkins Plan. (Fred had arrived at the house Lola shared with her brand-new husband, Emmett, and unpacked a Sam's Club block of cheddar from his suitcase.) And as long as he was single, Lola was afraid he would continue to show up unannounced, leaving her feeling unnerved and discombobulated.

It was a slow afternoon at the Second Chance Humane Society and Thrift Shop, where Lola volunteered twice a week, so she scanned the classified ads for dates. Unfortunately, all the women seemed to be looking for more. Fred was handsome, it was true, but he certainly wasn't "successful" or even "self-sufficient." He wasn't "romantic" or "a good listener." As far as Lola could tell, he had been kicked out of his third wife's house with little more than his fancy leather loafers.

"Some guys are going to get a *therapist,* sit around saying, 'What can I learn here, what went wrong, blah, blah,'" Fred had informed them the evening before, over a repast of cheese and cheese, "but not Fred Wilkerson!"

"And what do you plan to do?" asked Emmett.

"Forge ahead," said Fred. "What the hell do you think, Emmett?" Lola's father pronounced her husband's name with an ironic sneer, as if Emmett's name alone was an affront to manhood. When Emmett went into the kitchen, Fred muttered, "Face Man." Lola knew this was an insult, but she wasn't sure what it meant—that Emmett had a good-looking face? She knew it had something to do with being effeminate, which Emmett was not. Fred thought that anyone in academia—or "that ivory tower," as he put it—was a pussy.

Emmett was finishing up his PhD in geology. He came back from the field with a cooler of fresh-caught trout. He could make a fire from two sticks, fix appliances, and build furniture. He was taciturn, yes, and sometimes he went to his site and lost track of the time. More interested in rocks than Lola? Perhaps. But he was not a pussy.

"Forge ahead," said Emmett thoughtfully.

"The world is my oyster," said Fred. "I don't even have to commute to the Big Apple. Computers, the Web, what have you . . . you can telecommute from anywhere." Lola bit her fingernail, and did not mention that Fred had lost his last legitimate job in 1985, when she was thirteen years old.

"He *is* sober," whispered Lola, huddled close to Emmett in bed. Fred's snores ricocheted through the house.

"Okay," said Emmett reasonably.

"So that's something," said Lola. "I mean, I really respect him for that."

"That's great," Emmett agreed.

"I know he can't stay here," said Lola. Emmett was silent. "But I mean, he's lost everything. . . ."

"What happened?"

"I'm sure it was his fault," Lola sighed.

"It does seem possible," said Emmett.

"A few days?" said Lola.

"A week," said Emmett.

"You're wonderful," said Lola.

"I really don't think he belongs in Ouray," said Emmett.

"Do I?" said Lola.

"For a while longer, right?" said Emmett, pulling her close. "Just stay a while longer," he said.

In the morning, the kitchen was thick with a fug of cigar smoke. Fred was sitting in his bathrobe drinking coffee. Lola was taken aback at the sight of him: this was the same navy blue bathrobe with red piping that he had worn when she was a girl, before he had moved out and drunk himself into a coma.

"Dad," said Lola, "you know, it might be good if you'd smoke outside."

Fred shook his head. "Too cold," he said. "Christ, it's cold."

At eight thousand feet, it was chilly in the mornings. But Lola and Emmett's neighbor, Louise, was already watering her plants with a hose, her frail frame covered by an old wool coat.

"I mean seriously," said Emmett, shaving in the bathroom. "Seriously, Lola? I'm going to be sick."

"You smoke," said Lola, pointing at him with her toothbrush. She loved the sight of him in his boxer shorts, shaving cream up to his cute ears.

"I have like one Camel Light," said Emmett, "when I'm drunk. Maybe two." They kept a pack of cigarettes on a wrought-iron table outside the back door, and had spent warm and even cold evenings during their month together on rusty folding chairs, sipping beer and using an ashtray stolen from the Las Vegas Lounge, where Emmett had spun Lola around the dance floor.

"Seven," muttered Lola. She finished brushing her teeth and hair and followed him to the bedroom, where he was putting on his miner outfit. One of his part-time jobs while he finished his dissertation was giving historical tours through the old mine shafts. "I'm sorry," she said, sitting on the unmade bed. Then she stood, and started to pull the sheets up.

"It's just . . . cigars?" said Emmett.

"I'll talk to him about it," said Lola.

Emmett nodded. He put on his miner hat and left.

At the Humane Society, two other volunteers, both single women in their forties, wanted to hear all about Lola's father. "He's unemployed," said Lola. "He's sleeping on the couch. He's not the nicest." Lola tried to think of something wonderful to say about her father. "He is very smart," she said, finally.

"What color hair?" said Jayne, leaning against a cage, stirring honey into her teacup. Blueberry Muffin, a small tabby, reached his paw toward Jayne's hand. Jayne turned to Blueberry Muffin and smiled.

"Brown," said Lola.

"Dyed, or has he still got all his own?" asked Margie-Ann, who was cleaning the litter boxes.

"All his own," said Lola.

"I want to meet him," concluded Margie-Ann, pointing the scooper at Lola.

"He does sound interesting," agreed Jayne.

That evening, Fred opined that he would like to take a mine tour. "I'd give my right arm to see Emmett here off his golden pedestal," was how he put it. Emmett chewed slowly, and swallowed. They were eating a vegetable lasagna Lola had made that afternoon, frying eggplant slices in hot oil until her eyes smarted. Her mother had sent *The New Basics Cookbook,* and Lola was attempting to be domestic.

After a sip of his milk, Emmett said, "Well, Fred, the tours are every hour, on the half hour."

"How about a private tour?" said Fred.

"I don't think so, sir," said Emmett.

"Cut it with the 'sir'!" barked Fred.

"Guess what?" said Lola. "I'm planning a potluck with some friends from the Humane Society!"

"Whoop-de-doo," said Fred. He pulled a cigar from his front pocket.

"Some of the other volunteers are single," hinted Lola.

"Christ, a bunch of animal lovers," said Fred, shaking his head. "Who in the hell would want—" He stopped, just in time. Lola had a flash of memory: her father kicking her childhood cat, Bobby, making him squeal.

"I'm an animal lover," said Emmett. He winked at Lola sweetly.

"My daughter wouldn't be volunteering at a *cat shelter*," said Fred, "if you hadn't dragged her to godforsaken . . ." He opened his palm, encompassing the living room, the town of Ouray, the state of Colorado.

"It's just temporary," said Lola. Last spring, with her newly minted degree in journalism, she had accepted a job at the Cleveland *Plain Dealer,* due to start in the fall. After packing up her house and sending her belongings on a moving van to Ohio, she had left her cat, Sue, with her academic advisor and signed up for a raft trip down the Grand Canyon.

Lola hated sleeping outside. She was a suburban girl, after all. The heat, bugs, and enormous canyon walls made her nervous, and she drank deeply from the bottle of Jim Beam one of their two river guides, Hugh, passed around the camp-fire. It was clear on the first night that he was the gregarious one; the other guide, Emmett, introduced himself, talked a bit about the geology of the canyon, and retired early, heading away from the circle with a smile and a wave. He was an egghead, said Hugh, a brilliant scientist.

Lola woke at dawn. Her tent smelled like a whiskey distillery and her mouth tasted of the Beenie Weenies they'd eaten for dinner. At the edge of the rushing river, Lola saw a figure. She approached: it was Emmett, sipping coffee from a plastic mug with an owl on it and writing in his waterproof field book. "Hey," said Lola, sitting next to him.

"Coffee?"

"Thank you." Emmett poured from his thermos into the small metal top, and handed the cup to Lola. She peered at his notebook, and he smiled. "I double-checked the equipment," he said. "Now I'm just jotting down some"—he closed the book shyly—"some thoughts."

"I'm nervous," said Lola. "I'm from New York."

"I've never been there," said Emmett. This was amazing to Lola—who had never been to New York? He squinted against the rising sun, but did not say more. Lola leaned back on her elbows and crossed her ankles. Emmett had a spray of freckles across his face, sand-colored hair, and bright green eyes. Lola watched the river, next to Emmett. She wanted him to kiss her.

The trip was by turns deadly dull and terrifying. Hot days of floating were punctuated by shocking rapids, which Hugh and Emmett handled with panache, calling out for the boats to paddle or turn. While Lola's fellow rafters told competing stories by the campfire, Lola watched Emmett, who spent the evenings sipping beer quietly. More often than not, he'd steal off to read by himself, or go for an evening hike.

On the second-to-last day of the trip, Emmett asked Lola if she wanted to try a kayak. They were unstable; Lola declined. "I'll go right next to you," he said. "You can do it."

"No," said Lola, "I don't think I can."

She spent the day in a raft, wishing she had been more courageous. Millie, an ophthalmologist from Idaho, proclaimed that kayaking was the most exciting thing she'd ever done. "All the water, churning and broiling . . . it's like a life force, you know?"

"You mean *roiling*?" asked Lola.

"Roiling, broiling, whatever," said Millie, adjusting her floppy sun hat. "It's better than sex."

That night, after everyone was asleep, Lola walked to Emmett's tent. His lamp was on, so she pulled the flap back. "I wanted to thank you for . . . for the trip," she said. "And I'm mad at myself. I wanted to try the kayak, but I was too scared." He closed his book—it was a spy novel. "Come in," he said.

"Also, I wanted to kiss you," said Lola.

"Come here," said Emmett.


The next morning, Lola pulled the neoprene skirt over her thighs and climbed into a kayak. Emmett helped her launch into the water. Navigating the boat at water level was thrilling: the speed awed Lola, and the way the small boat responded to the tiniest calibration of her paddle. Nonetheless, when Millie approached her at lunchtime and said, "See what I'm saying?" Lola shrugged.

"Millie," she said, the memory of Emmett's warm caress vivid in her mind, "the kayak's great, but I'm going to have to disagree with you."

After climbing ashore at Lake Mead and taking their first showers in weeks, Emmett and Lola drove to the Las Vegas Lounge to go dancing. Emmett dipped Lola and said, in her ear, "You're gorgeous."

He pulled her back to her feet, and she laced her arms around him. "You say that to all the rafters," she said. His chest was broad and slim: in his arms, she felt serene.

"No," said Emmett.

"Buy me some tequila, will you?" said Lola.

In short: they were married in the middle of the night. The memory is hazy, but happy, in her mind. At Cupid's Chapel, Lola became Mrs. Emmett Chase. When she woke up with a brutal hangover and a cheap band on her finger, Emmett was watching her, propped on one elbow. "Well," he said, "isn't this an interesting development."

Lola blinked. "I'm moving to Cleveland in six weeks," she said.

Emmett nodded. "How about staying in Colorado until then?" he asked.

So Lola put her duffel bag in Emmett's truck. As they drove nine hours to Ouray, a small town in the southwest corner of the state, Lola decided that she'd stay with Emmett for a few weeks, what the hell, then pick up her cat and move to Cleveland. The marriage could always be annulled.

Emmett told her about growing up as the eldest son of a wealthy Texas oil family. Geology, Emmett said, had once been a pursuit of discovering the past—trying to figure out the history of the landscape—but now encompassed everything from the mountaintops to the oil underneath the ground. There was a fringe group of wild geologists, Emmett said, who were arguing that humans had so altered the planet they'd started a new epoch. "There was the Ice Age," he said, speaking animatedly, "then the Holocene, which is now, and these guys are proposing the new era be called the Anthropocene, from the Greek *anthropos,* which means 'man,' and *ceno,* 'new.' "

"Altered it how?" asked Lola.

"Global warming," said Emmett. "Disturbing the carbon cycle. Ocean acidification. Changing erosion patterns. Wholesale changes to plant and animal life . . ."

"Jesus, just stop," said Lola. "You're depressing me."

"I think it's exciting," said Emmett. "I mean, yeah, you can see it as sad, but you can also see it as an opportunity. Patterns can be altered."

Emmett had applied for jobs everywhere from New Jersey to Saudi Arabia. "I've been all over the western U.S., but I've never lived abroad. There are so many places I want to see," he said.

His enthusiasm made Lola realize how little excitement she held for her future at *The Plain Dealer.* It occurred to her that she had never studied anything she could hold in her hand.

"Listen, Fred," said Emmett, "if you want a private tour, I'll give you a private tour. How about it?"

Fred was busy inhaling in quick breaths, trying to light his cigar.

"That sounds great, Emmett," said Lola. "How about Sunday?"

"You got it," said Emmett.

"Sunday it is," said Fred, filling his mouth and the house with smoke. He puffed for a while, Emmett and Lola staring at him, and then he said, "Never been in a mine, I've got to say."

After dinner, Fred said, "I suppose you want to hear about the demise of my latest. It all began with an unfortunate blonde named Winnie."

"You know what, Dad? I don't really want to hear this."

"Well, okay then," said Fred. "Now that I think about it, it's none of your fucking business."

"If you're going to talk to my . . . to my Lola that way," said Emmett, "I'm going to have to ask you to leave, sir."

"With pleasure," said Fred. He stood, brushed off his pants, and made for the door. "About *time*," he said, "for a nightcap."

This was what Fred did, his modus operandi. He fell off the wagon and blamed it on someone else. He was never at fault, just an upstanding man pushed to the brink by a wife, a daughter, the world conspiring against him. It was so discouraging. Whenever Lola said good-bye to her father, she wondered if she would ever see him again.

Every time she moved, Lola picked a postcard and sent it to Fred, carefully writing her change of address. At the V & S Variety Store, she had found a card with a picture of a flock of sheep and written, "Dear Dad, My new address is below. Hope you are well." Lola stood with her ballpoint poised for some time. She almost wrote "love" before her name, but then refrained. She did love her father—desperately—but knew that she shouldn't, after what he had done, and who he had turned out to be. Finally, she scribbled, "All best, LOLA." The front of the card read, MISSING EWE!

Now, Lola said, "Don't leave, Dad. Really, it's fine. Stay."

Fred shrugged and, as if he were doing them a favor, sat down in a faded blue La-Z-Boy chair. Relieved, Lola looked at Emmett, who was considering her with something she had never seen before in his eyes: disappointment.

Margie-Ann said she thought a mine tour would be even better than a potluck. "It'll be *intriguing*," said Margie-Ann. Jayne, whose father had worked in the mines for thirty years, was noncommittal. She might be busy, she said, she really wasn't sure. But when they pulled into the parking lot on Sunday morning, both Jayne and Margie-Ann were waiting for them, wearing dresses.

"Do you two have any more comfortable shoes?" Emmett asked politely. Lola's friends looked down at their fancy footwear and smiled, shaking their heads. Fred turned on the charm, joking about carrying the ladies across the threshold and feigning interest in the animal adoption process. Emmett waited patiently, hands in his Patagonia parka.

When Fred had finished schmoozing, he said, "Face Man! Let's get this show on the road."

Emmett gave everyone a hard hat and a yellow rain slicker, and they climbed into the mine car. Emmett went into the office to get the key, and Fred turned to Lola. He was handsome, spirited underneath his plastic hat. "Don't know what to tell you, honey," he said, putting his arm around Lola and pulling her close. He was wearing his cologne, Royall Lyme. He smelled like the successful banker he had once been. "I just think you could do better, I don't know what else to say," said Fred.

Emmett came out of the office, holding up a ring of keys. "Are we ready to take a ride back in time?" he asked. Lola, who had never been on a mine tour, was suddenly nervous.

"Move it along," said Fred. He squeezed her again. Margie-Ann and Jayne turned to Lola, making apprehensive-but-game faces. "Don't worry about a thing, ladies," said Fred.

Emmett opened the wooden doors, exposing a dark tunnel. He climbed into the mine car and drove slowly forward. Inside the shaft, the air was clammy and close. Lola felt as if she couldn't get enough oxygen. "We're going to head eighteen hundred feet into Gold Hill," Emmett began. "At the height of the mining boom in the San Juan mountains, thousands worked underground."

Lola knew that these shafts collapsed, trapping miners

who simply suffocated one by one. She had heard stories about these men, and now she felt their presence. She had never had an anxiety attack, but perhaps she was about to. Emmett began talking about dynamiting and methods of gold extraction. Fred's arm around Lola was a comfort.

"My poor dad," whispered Jayne, peering around.

"This is eerie," said Margie-Ann.

"You said it," said Fred.

Emmett stopped his spiel mid-sentence. After a moment, he said, in a controlled voice, "Does anyone want to hear about the history of the mine?"

"Is there anything titillating?" said Fred, chuckling. "Maybe we could skip ahead to that part."

Margie-Ann giggled guiltily. "I think history is fascinating," said Jayne.

"The miners worked twelve-hour days," said Emmett. His voice was calm and lovely, if a bit strident. "They went to work in the dark and came home in the dark. Their lives were at risk, but they did what they had to do to support their wives and children."

There was a whispering sound, a match against a matchbox. Fred had taken his arm from around Lola's shoulders and was bent over, lighting a cigar. He made the puffing, inhaling sound, and then said, "Ah," as the cigar filled his mouth and the mine shaft with smoke.

"Fred, you're going to have to put that out," said Emmett. There was an uncomfortable silence. Lola wanted to climb from the car and run back toward the entrance.

"Fred," said Emmett, standing up. He trained his head-lamp on Lola's father. "Fred, I said *put that out.*"

"Why not just put out the cigar," said Margie-Ann, nervously.

"Come on, Fred," said Jayne. Lola felt a wave of sadness for them, imagining the anticipation with which they had put on dresses and shoes with heels. She could almost smell their wishes souring.

"Dad . . . ," said Lola.

"What?" said Fred. "What is it, Lollabee?" This was the name he had used for Lola when she was little, when they had watched *Sesame Street* together in their Upper East Side apartment, Fred dressed for work but lingering, letting Lola sit on his lap and saying, "What letter is that, Lollabee? Is that the letter 'J'?"

But Lola didn't say anything. She looked at Emmett pleadingly, though she wasn't sure what her plea was. End this, or fix this—help me. Fred continued to puff.

With the same sure movements Emmett had used on the river, he stepped from the mine car and walked to Lola's father. He took the cigar out of Fred's hand and tossed it to the ground, extinguishing it with the heel of his boot. "Now," he said, "let me tell you about the day they discovered gold in the Bachelor mine."

"Oh my," said Jayne.

Fred chuckled meanly, shaking his head. "Oh, this is ripe," he said. "This is really ripe. You know what, Face Man? I'd like an apology, or I'm going to just walk right out of here."

Emmett cocked his head, and put his hands on his hips. "Adios," he said.

Fred sat up straight. "Lola," he said sharply. "Honey, I'm not standing for this. It's about time to skedaddle. I'm going. Come on."

He stood, and exited the car. He took Lola's hand, gripping her fingers painfully. Lola was amazed to find that it took only a quick shake to free herself. She wasn't leaving until her husband had finished the story of the Bachelor. And she wasn't moving to Cleveland.

## Motherhood and Terrorism

Lola thought the baby shower would be canceled due to the beheading, but she was wrong. Karen McDaniels called early Friday morning to see if Lola wanted a ride to Liberty Avenue.

"Oh," said Lola, "is your shower still on?"

"Well, why wouldn't it be?" said Karen, an argumentative edge to her voice.

"The attacks in al-Khobar," said Lola, "and . . . and the head." She swallowed. "I guess I thought . . ."

"Did you know him?" said Karen.

"What? No."

"Phew!" Karen breathed a sigh of relief. "Honey," she

said, her voice slipping back into its buttery Texas twang, "it's all quiet now up there. You can't let these Muslim whack jobs run your life."

"Right," said Lola.

"And Jody's making nachos," added Karen.

"Okay," said Lola, hanging up the phone.

Emmett looked up from the *Arab News*. "Who was that?" he asked.

"Karen," said Lola, "of Karen and Andy McDaniels."

"Great!" said Emmett, flashing a wide smile before looking back at the paper. On the top of his head, his hair was thinning a little. Lola remembered lying next to him soon after they had begun living together, looking at his sandy hair and thinking she owned every handful of it. Now she understood: she would lose it all eventually, and be left with a big, bald head.

"What's in the news?" said Lola.

"Oh," said Emmett, "same old."

Lola knew that the shooting spree on the nearby Oasis Compound was not same old. Twenty-two people had been killed, and the terrorists had promised to rid the Arabian peninsula of infidels. Infidels like Lola. She had been dreaming of gunmen for weeks. In her dreams, a man with a scratchy beard held her head against his chest. He asked her whether she was Christian or Muslim. When she said she was an atheist, but willing to be convinced, the terrorist looked confused. Then he shot her.

·   ·   ·

From the moment she'd stepped off the plane—her back sore from the sixteen-hour flight, her eyes blinded by desert sun—she had felt a brewing dread. It was cool on the tarmac, and she found out later that the whole zone was air-conditioned.

"They air-condition the *outside?*" she'd said to Emmett.

"They've got more money than you can imagine," said Emmett. "They do whatever they please."

Day by day, fear had grown in Lola. At the welcoming cocktail parties, the compound softball games, she approached other wives, asking them, *Are you afraid?* And: *Do you ever wonder if we should go home?* She found quickly that these were not the sorts of questions you asked in Haven Compound.

"You sweet thing," Karen McDaniels had said, moving her hand from her young daughter's shoulder to Lola's cheek. "You need some hobbies and a little baby or two. And a drink. Somebody get this girl a drink!" Karen, who was probably Lola's age, was pregnant with her third child.

"You're my wonderful Lola, that's who you are," said Emmett in bed one night, when Lola had drunk duty-free wine until she couldn't keep from talking. Emmett scratched her back and said, "Maybe take some tennis lessons?"

"Tennis lessons? Ugh," she said, thinking of her mother, a tennis pro in Westchester. At sixty, Nan still wore short white skirts. Her exposed legs had always embarrassed Lola, and the way she stretched on the court, fully aware all the husbands were watching her.

"I've never felt so *lost,*" said Lola.

"Oh sweetie," said Emmett, "yes you have."

. . .

Now, he drained his coffee cup. "Off to the races," he said, glancing at his beeper. The damn beeper woke them up nights, paging Emmett to discuss some drilling mishap. When it went off, Emmett ran to the office as if he were a doctor, though what he worked on was not hearts, but oil wells.

"What races?" said Lola.

"I don't know," said Emmett, looking embarrassed. "Just something to say."

"My mom wrote again," said Lola. "She says we're not safe here. She thinks we should come home."

Emmett put his thumb and forefinger to his eyes and pressed, a gesture that made him look old. "We're safe," he said. "I don't know how many ways to say it. But if you need to go to your mom's for a while, then you should go."

"I have Karen's baby shower today," said Lola.

"That will be fun," said Emmett, "won't it?"

"Sure," said Lola.

"Maybe we should have a baby," said Emmett.

"Spare me," said Lola.

She stood in front of her bedroom mirror for some time. The master suite had thick carpeting and carved mahogany furniture. It was a bedroom fit for a sultan, with gold braiding and tassels around everything, even the Kleenex-box holder. When Lola lay on her bed, she tried to understand how she had ended up an oil wife beneath a garish chandelier.

"Are you afraid to be here?" she asked Corazon, the maid scrubbing her Jacuzzi tub.

Corazon did not answer. Lola pulled on a black dress her mother had sent from Old Navy. It smelled of America: crisp, synthetic, clean.

"Corazon?" Lola said. "Are you afraid to be on an American compound?"

Corazon stood up, her hand on her back, and pursed her lips. She looked at the floor as she said, "You are a target, Mrs. Lola, and I am in the way of the target."

"Fabulous," said Lola.

Nan had e-mailed four more times, saying she was very worried and would pay for Lola's flight to JFK if money was the problem. Lola thought of her mother waiting outside Baggage Claim in her aging Mercedes, a visor stuck in her platinum hair. She thought of her mother's smug smile, the way she would not say, *You thought you found love, but men are all the same.*

"They say we are protected," Lola typed back. "The attacks are on the coast, and the compound is filled with guards. I am headed to a friend's baby shower! Love, Lola."

Lola clicked SEND, then held her head in her hands.

"Miss," said Mayala, the cook, tapping Lola on the shoulder. "Miss, your lunch is ready." Lola nodded and wiped her eyes. She turned to face Mayala, a thin woman with her hair pulled severely back from her face. "I made you the frozen pizza," she said, not hiding her disgust. "The Tombstone frozen pizza," she added.

"I appreciate it," said Lola.

As she chewed the slices, Lola looked around her gleaming kitchen. Just a year before, they had lived in a one-bedroom rental in Colorado. Lola sat behind the front desk at the Second Chance Humane Society and Thrift Shop, and Emmett ran raft trips and gave tours through the local mines. They made simple dinners on a hot plate and watched the stars from their front porch. Lola's cat, Sue, loved the porch; Sue was now living indefinitely with Emmett's parents.

Finding abandoned puppies in a box outside the front door of the Humane Society was horrible, of course, but Lola was the one who got to bring them inside, and give them breakfast. She was allowed to name a rescued cat, a brown short-hair someone had found at the Orvis Hot Springs. ("Nudie.") The only part of her job she couldn't stand was interacting with the people ditching their pets. She tried not to look at the animal's faces as their owners made lame excuses about having to move out-of-state or feeling the pet would be better off in a quieter home. Lola stroked the dogs, settled the cats into her lap. She met the animals' curious gazes directly when their owners had departed. "I'm glad you're here," she told them.

After a year, Emmett finished his dissertation. Three job offers materialized: a one-year postdoc in Connecticut, an assistant professor position in a rural town somewhat near Raleigh, and a geophysicist job with British Petroleum in

Saudi Arabia. "I look around at my professors and they just seem so *bored*," he'd said. "In Saudi, I'll be working with the best scientists, and the fact is we all use gas. Like it or not. Even professors use gas, Lolly. And BP will send us all over the world." Emmett's hands had moved like birds as he described the adventurous life that awaited them. "We'll never worry about money again. We'll have maids. A cook, even!" Emmett came from an oil family—his father had done stints in Libya and Saudi—so he knew whereof he spoke.

"I'm not worried about money now," said Lola. In fact, she liked their cozy house and mismatched silverware. It all felt so different from her miserable childhood, though she had to admit that Saudi Arabia would feel different too.

One night, Emmett made lamb kebabs with Middle Eastern spices and placed a handmade card next to her plate. *Will you come with me to Riyadh?* the card read. When Lola said yes, Emmett popped a bottle of champagne.

Andrei, the veterinarian who volunteered at Second Chance, was nonplussed by the news of her move. "I thought you might stick around a while," he said.

"I'm sorry," said Lola. "Emmett finished his PhD. He took a job in Saudi Arabia. It's just for a few years. I'm going to write about the Middle East. Or a novel. I'm going to write something, is the plan. I was a communications major." Lola realized she was rambling, and fell silent.

"Oh," said Andrei dismissively. "Well . . . sounds wild." And it had sounded wild, at first. Lola imagined nights of hot sex in some sort of bedouin tent.

.   .   .

As Lola ate, she saw that Mayala, usually a frenzy of activity, was standing still in the kitchen. Mayala had seven children at home, but spent her days in Haven, cooking for Lola and Emmett. Often, Emmett worked late, and Lola sat alone at the long table with platters of food. She could hear her Filipino staff giggling and speaking rapid Tagalog in the kitchen, but she did not dare to join them.

"Is something wrong?" Lola asked Mayala.

"No ma'am," said Mayala, but she did not meet Lola's eyes.

In two days, she would be gone, writing on the kitchen dry erase board, "I am sorry. I am scared. Cook pizza for twenty minutes at 350 degrees."

After lunch, Lola went for a walk. Haven was surrounded by high walls, so she could walk outside without a head covering or long pants. The pool was filled with kids, and two teenage girls lay on either side of a boom box playing Aerosmith. As Lola walked by, one of them lifted an arm and pressed her fingers to her skin, checking her tan. Standing by the pool were two armed Saudi men dressed in guard uniforms, their sunglasses hiding their eyes.

Suzi and Fran waved as Lola passed the tennis courts. As doubles partners, they won every tournament. Suzi's husband, Carl, was Haven's best golfer. Emmett had encouraged Lola to get out, make friends, but it was so gut-wrenchingly hot. She preferred to read inside her cool bedroom, and had joined the Bookies only to shut Emmett up. The first book choice had been *Ten Stupid Things Women Do to Mess Up*

*Their Lives,* by Dr. Laura Schlessinger. Women were not allowed to drive outside of the compound, so Lola arranged for
a chauffeur to take her shopping in the city. This was before
the Khobar massacre, and Lola was nervous, but excited, to
leave the compound.

As soon as the limousine passed through the guard station, the landscape changed. Abruptly, green lawns and large
houses were replaced by desert. The limousine, clean and
black as they left the compound, became covered with a thin
layer of sand as they moved toward the city. They drove
through narrow streets, and Lola saw groups of women in
robes led by men who walked a few strides ahead of them.
Some of the women held hands, and Lola felt a pang of jeal-
ousy. Lola had never had a group of giggling girlfriends. She
had always been the one in the corner of the bar, staring at her
napkin.

The limousine passed fast-food restaurants—McDonald's,
Kentucky Fried Chicken—and Lola saw the separate en-
trances for women and men. Stopped at a traffic light, Lola
watched three boys playing with a thin dog that looked like
some sort of Doberman mix. The dog rolled over, exposing
its stomach, and one of the boys shrieked and knelt down,
pressing his face to the dog's neck. There were flies everywhere, flies that had somehow been exterminated from
Haven.

Lola walked around the bookstore for an hour, hiding
under her *abaya*. From the eye opening, she watched other
women touching each other, pressing fingers to the thick
cloth. Lola could not bring herself to buy the Bookies' pick,

and bought *All Creatures Great and Small* instead with her wad of riyals. A month later, the Oasis Compound was attacked, and people started ordering books online.

The baby shower was at four. Corazon made Lola sit down, then rubbed blush into Lola's cheeks. At the Humane Society, Andrei used to sing whenever Lola walked past his office: *"Her name was Lola, she was a showgirl!"* Life was simpler then, before Lola knew she should be ashamed of her bare legs, her car, and her country. She couldn't help it: Lola started to cry.

"I don't understand you, madame," said Corazon.

"My mom wants me to come home," said Lola. "I don't know what to do. Maybe she's right."

"How about this nice headband?" said Corazon, taking the plastic band from her own head.

"No, no," said Lola, but Corazon did not listen, sweeping Lola's red hair back, jamming the band in place.

"Maybe everyone should stay home," said Corazon. "Maybe everyone should stay at their own home and never leave." Lola looked at Corazon, whose home was the Philippines. "Wear the nice headband," Corazon said, staring at Lola and speaking in a cold hiss.

Emmett was excelling at his job—he was addicted to the frenzy, to his own growing importance—and his desire for a baby seemed to grow with every successful well. "Don't you want children?" he'd say over dinner.

"Someday!" cried Lola. "I'm busy," she said, pointing to

the second bedroom, which they called her office. She sat in her office for hours every morning, drinking coffee and surfing the Internet on her new computer. Emmett had made a sign that said, QUIET PLEASE, NOVELIST AT WORK," and taped it to the door. But Lola was sick of trying to write. She didn't want to report the news, and she didn't want to make things up. She had thought of blogging about her expat experience, but after one entry, "Desert Dessert," about the sweets she'd eaten (saffron tapioca and Arabian orange ice were her favorites, so far), she had run out of steam.

"My mom always said the compounds were a great place for kids," said Emmett.

"That was a different time," said Lola. "It was safe here then."

"And she was a different person," said Emmett.

"What's that supposed to mean?"

"I don't know what to do to make you happy," said Emmett.

"How about kissing me?"

He swept her up and carried her into their palace of a bedroom. He kissed her, and then she went into the bathroom and inserted her diaphragm.

Jody, who was throwing the baby shower, had a month-old infant named Rebecca. Karen and Jody had tried to get pregnant at the same time, Karen had told Lola, but "Andy's swimmers were a little slow." Lola laughed uncomfortably, hoping she would not be expected to talk about her husband's sperm.

Karen knocked on Jody's door, and Jody pulled it open forcefully. "Karen's here!" she screamed. Lola followed Karen, resplendent in a pink maternity dress, down Jody's long front hallway to the living room, where twenty or so suntanned women sat on leather couches. In the adjoining playroom, kids of all ages and their Filipino nannies watched *Shrek*.

"Hooray!" said Suzi, who had changed from her tennis whites into a dress printed with fuchsia crabs. Suzi and Lola were among the few Haven wives who were not from Texas. Suzi had decided to pretend Saudi was Nantucket.

"Do you want a drink?" asked Karen. Lola shook her head.

"Oh, come on," said Jody, "it's my bathtub special." Lola shrugged, and Jody ladled her an icy glass.

"Sit back now, make yourself at home," said Jody, leading Lola to a La-Z-Boy. Jody had returned to her trim size two in a matter of weeks, it seemed. Lola watched the hubbub, sipping her drink and eating whatever hors d'oeuvres Jody's maids brought by: deviled eggs, shrimp, nachos. She listened to the women talk about the stupidity of having to wear an *abaya* outside the compound. "For the Arabs," said Suzi, "your hair is like your boobs."

"At the mall yesterday, I saw someone with a few curls sticking out," noted Jody.

"That's like wearing a skimpy bikini," said Beth gravely.

"That's like wearing a thong!" said Suzi.

"You went to the mall yesterday?" said Lola. As soon as she said it, she wished she had not.

"Sorry?" Jody looked at Lola, narrowing her eyes.

"I mean, should we be leaving the compound?" Since the massacre, Lola's stomach hurt from the time Emmett left the house until the moment she heard his car returning at the end of the day.

Karen sighed. "Lola," she said, "you can either think about the nutters all day long or you can go about your business."

"That's true," said Suzi. She crossed one long leg over the other.

"Has it been this bad before?" said Lola. There was a silence.

Beth Landings ladled herself another cup of gin. "No," she said simply. "I've been here for ten years, and this is the worst. To be completely honest, I'm scared to death."

"We might go to Bahrain," admitted an older woman. "I'm sick of this . . . this fiasco," she said. "The Saudis can't control the terrorists anymore. Maybe they don't even want to."

"They just shot people," said Beth quietly. "They just stormed Oasis Compound and shot people in the head."

No one spoke, and finally Jody rose and clapped her hands. "Time for the games!" she cried, her face brilliant and brave.

The first game was the string game. Jody made Karen stand up, and each woman cut a length of string that estimated Karen's girth. Hilarity ensued: every single person thought Karen was wider than she was.

The I-Spy game was a silver tray filled with baby items.

Jody let them look at the tray for a few minutes, and then she covered it with a sheet. Lola chewed her pencil eraser, trying to remember what was on the tray as the kitchen timer ticked. *"Diaper,"* wrote Lola, *"Rattle, Teddy Bear, Bottle."* In truth, she didn't even know what half the items were. Beth won the I-Spy game, remembering seventeen items, including the rectal thermometer.

As Karen opened each present, the women made comments—"A Godsend," for example, when she opened the Diaper Genie, or "Alice couldn't get enough of that damn toy," when she opened the Lazy-Bee Singing Mobile. Lola tried to imagine her own child dressed in the appealing clothes, batting the mobile. Surprisingly, the thought made her happy. Would her future baby have Emmett's green eyes, his slow, sweet smile? Lola hoped so.

Lola saw a guard through the window. He was looking straight at her, his hand on his gun. What if he was a terrorist? *Look at that American, enjoying deviled eggs and nachos!* she imagined the man thinking. *What does she believe in, I'd like to know.* When he saw her looking, the guard nodded and moved on.

Twice during the party, Lola caught herself running her hand along her neck, pressing at the tendons and the bones.

Outside Lola's house, Karen put her car in park. "Francis is home with the girls," said Karen. "Mind if I come in for a few?"

"Sure," said Lola, surprised. Corazon seemed happy to

have a guest, and brought out a tray of lemonade and cookies. Karen sank into one of Lola's sofas.

"Well, did you have fun?" asked Karen.

"I did," said Lola. "I really did."

"You know," said Karen, "a million years ago, I was in advertising."

"Sorry?" said Lola.

Karen played with her hair. "You think I'm some dumb housewife," said Karen. "Don't look so shocked. I know."

"I don't . . . ," said Lola.

"You think you're smarter than everybody else," said Karen. "You think you can figure out what's going on out there." She pointed to the window. "I'm here to tell you, sweetie, at some point you have to stop asking questions. This is your life, Lola. This is your house. It's pretty nice, don't you think?"

"You know," said Lola, "I've got to get dinner started. . . ."

"Let me finish my piece," said Karen. She leaned toward Lola. "I promise you, what's going on in here," she pointed to her pregnant belly, "is a hell of a lot more meaningful than what a bunch of Muslim nut jobs might be planning. You mark my words."

"I'm miserable," said Lola, realizing the truth even as she spoke.

Karen stopped talking, her mouth open.

"I don't feel safe here," said Lola, "and I've almost forgotten who I wanted to be."

Karen looked down at her swollen hands, and Lola could

practically hear the indignation draining out of her. "Holy guacamole," said Karen.

"I don't think I'm smarter," said Lola. "I'm just sad."

"You know, I was drifting until Babs came along," said Karen, thoughtfully. "Then it all came clear."

"That sounds nice," said Lola.

"It's real nice," said Karen. Then she said, kindly, "Honey?"

"What?"

"You've got to have faith in something. Think about that before you jump on Lufthansa."

"I will," said Lola.

"And thank you for the lemonade," said Karen Mc-Daniels. She stood, clutching her lower back. "Andy better get his boy this time," she said, grimacing.

When Emmett got home from work that night, Lola met him at the door. "Hey," she said, "let's go out to dinner."

"Out to dinner?" said Emmett. He opened the passenger side of his car, gathered his briefcase.

"I'm sick of this big house," said Lola. "Remember when we used to go driving at night, just to see where we'd end up?"

Emmett sighed. He had grown pudgy from eating too much and sitting at his workstation. Even with the leather shoes and the Saab, though, Lola could still see in him the river guide who fly-fished along the Grand Canyon, his arm moving gracefully, a beer stuck in the top pocket of his waders.

"Okay, okay," he said, after a moment. "How about the Japanese place?"

"No," said Lola. "Out."

"The Mexican place?"

"You know what I mean, Emmett."

"Look," said Emmett, coming toward her. "It's nothing great out there. You've been out. You have to wear the—"

"The *abaya*. I know."

He set his face in a mask of calm. "Okay," he said. "All right," he said, "fine."

Emmett changed into clean clothes and Lola put on the long-sleeved black robe and headscarf. As they drove the Saab down the busy streets, Lola watched the men drinking tea outside dim cafés, the boys selling cigarettes. "We could have taken the bus," she said, "for a little change of pace." Emmett snorted.

"They hate us here, don't they?" said Lola.

"Of course they don't," said Emmett. Then he added, "Well, some of them do. A few crazy ones."

"More than a few," said Lola.

"You know," said Emmett, "I work with people who are very happy we're here. What I do matters to a lot of people."

Lola turned back to her husband. The anger she had nursed all day—maybe even for months—faded when she saw that he was biting back tears. "Emmett . . . ," she said.

"Can't you be proud of me?" he said, staring at the unpaved road, where a cow was trying to cross the street. "Can't you just try?"

The restaurant Emmett chose was a steak house, lit up

like a Christmas tree. When Lola noted this, Emmett told her to keep her voice down. They were seated at a table set elaborately for six. Next to them, a large Saudi family had already been served their dinner. The women scooped food underneath their headscarves politely. Lola watched them as she squeezed into a chair, but they took no notice of her.

"Come here," said Emmett. "You're three seats away. And wearing that damn hood."

Lola moved closer, and Emmett put his hand on the fabric covering her knee. "Should we drink from all the glasses?" he said. "Should we eat off all the plates?"

He was trying to be charming, and Lola smiled tightly. Not that Emmett could see. For all he knew, she was in tears underneath her headscarf.

They ordered filet mignon and Cokes. They talked about Karen's baby shower, the time they'd gone skydiving, how a well-done steak felt like the tip of your nose when pressed. Finally, Lola put down her knife and fork. "Emmett," she said, "we need to talk."

"Yeah," said Emmett, "I know."

"I just don't—," Lola began.

"Hold on," said Emmett. His eyes were the color of jade, with bursts of white around the irises. He blinked in the fluorescent light of the restaurant. There was something in his forehead, in the lines around his mouth: he was just as scared as she was. "You have to understand," he said. "I've been in school my whole life up till now. I'm doing complicated, exciting work, and I love it."

Lola glanced around at the Saudi families, the glassware, the lights. "I don't want to be here," she said. Lola thought about her father suddenly, understanding for the first time that he must have been trying to alleviate unbearable pain by abandoning them.

Emmett looked right at her. "If you need to go home," he said, "we'll go. I don't know what the hell I'll do for work, but okay. I'll quit. Is that what you want? I'll quit. There: I said it."

Lola did not feel joyful, as she had expected. She felt queasy, and excused herself. In the ladies' room, two Saudi women stood at the mirror. Above their dark bodies, their faces were bright, topped with elaborate hairdos. Precious stones glittered in their ears and around their necks. One applied very pink lipstick to her lips.

There was a couch in the corner, and Lola sat down. She felt calm underneath the robe, with no skin exposed. She could walk out of the restaurant and into the street, joining the groups of people out for an evening stroll. She could take a cab to the airport, and fly to JFK. Nobody would notice her: she was just a blank expanse of cloth in the shape of a woman.

Without warning, the lights in the bathroom went out. Lola heard her blood in her ears. The women at the mirror fell silent. As Lola's eyes adjusted to the darkness, she saw them putting their headscarves back on. They walked past Lola quickly, and she smelled perfume.

She was alone. At prayer time, they cut the electricity, she knew that. But she imagined a man in the doorway of the bathroom. She imagined cold metal against her temple, a blade to her throat. The man would take pictures of her, afterward. He would post a video on the Internet.

It occurred to Lola that if she and Emmett had a baby here, they could tell it the Jacuzzi tub was an indoor pool. A child would think Corazon loved it wholeheartedly, and not just because she was being paid. And when they were forced to evacuate (which they surely would be, sooner or later) the baby would know only that they were together—a family—and safe.

Though she felt far from home or a hope of home, she made her decision. She was putting her faith in something, and he was sitting at a big table, too upset to eat his buttery baked potato. As she walked back to her husband, Lola thought about lying on her expensive sheets and holding a baby—their baby—to her breast. To the baby, Lola would smell like a mother, and the ridiculous chandelier would look like stars.

# The Blue Flame

Sissy was allowed to visit when her first grandchild was six weeks old and the new family was falling apart. Emmett "had a big day at work" and nobody trusted Lola behind the wheel, so Sissy gamely took a taxi from the airport.

"What brings you to Austin?" said the taxi driver, a fat man with a porkpie hat and a biography of Buddha on the dashboard.

"My son just had a baby," said Sissy. "A baby named Louis."

"Nice name," said the driver, putting the car in gear and lurching toward the airport exit.

"I suppose," said Sissy. In truth, she thought the name was

pretentious and strange. Louis? With all the wonderful—
and masculine—names in her storied family, it bewildered
Sissy that her son had seemingly picked a name out of the
ether. (Emmett had been the name of Sissy's beloved father,
might he rest in peace.) "He just looks like a *Louis*," Emmett's wife, Lola, had said on the phone. "You know what I
mean?"

Sissy did not know. Furthermore, she thought this statement was ridiculous. A baby didn't look like anyone, not
for at least six months; this was Sissy's belief. But she
said, "Mmm!" to her daughter-in-law, and felt that saying
"Mmm!" was both supportive and not telling a lie.

Austin was about as hot as Midland, but much more
urban. As they whizzed along the highway, Sissy took in
the cranes, busy building the new condominium complexes
some of her friends were investigating. She was not the only
woman in Midland with grandchildren in Austin. Many
University of Texas grads never left, falling awkwardly into
some job or another. Sissy was very proud that her son had
gone east for college, west for a doctorate, dabbled in the oil
patch, and then returned to Texas as a triumphant (if poor)
professor. Her son, a professor! (Her second-born, a disaster,
but why dwell on the negative?) Sissy had loved mentioning
to friends that she was off to see her grandbaby in Austin,
which was the best city in Texas, especially if you were a tree-
hugger, as Emmett was.

The taxi deposited Sissy and her suitcase in front of a yellow house with green shutters. It was a real 1920s ginger-
bread house, Emmett had told her excitedly, on one of the

rare occasions he had telephoned. He and Lola had bought a subscription to *This Old House,* Emmett said, and they were talking about building a white picket fence and adding an outdoor shower.

Outdoor shower! This was before the baby, of course.

Sissy hadn't even finished paying the taxi driver when the front door slammed open and there was Lola, who had once been beautiful. Of course, she was still carrying extra weight, even at six weeks, but the poor thing seemed to have misplaced her lipstick and hairbrush as well. "Welcome!" called Lola, with desperate cheer. In her arms (a bit flabby—had the girl never heard of push-ups?), Louis screamed bloody murder.

"Heavens," said Sissy, feigning love, which she knew would come with time, "is that my very first grandbaby?"

Lola made a strangled assent and held the flailing infant toward Sissy, who quickly paid the driver, ran up the walkway, and took Louis in her arms. "Oh," she said, gazing at the red, angry face.

"Isn't he . . . ," said Lola. "Isn't he . . . wonderful? Can you hold him just for a sec while I run to the bathroom?"

"Of course, dear," said Sissy.

Lola's mother—her *single* mother, Nan—had been in Austin for Louis's birth. Nan had been invited for the big day, the naming, the happy homecoming, back when all the baby clothes were clean and the nursery did not yet smell like sour milk and diapers. And then, just as Lola began to go bonkers and Emmett had started to resent Lola and all of it, Nan flew back to her tennis pro life in New York and who was left to call? Sissy, and she'd come to town like a loyal mutt hungry for leftovers.

Sissy held her grandson on the sagging front porch, keeping an eye on her suitcase. A girl in a tank top wandered by, holding a poodle on a red leash. A man on a strange bicycle pedaled past. A boy parked an old Ford Fairlane in front of Emmett and Lola's house, got out of the car, and put on sunglasses. The baby kept screaming. Sissy supposed she should do something.

"Oh, thank you," said Lola, coming back outside, still clad in a nightgown over sweatpants. "Do you want me to get your suitcase?" said Lola. "Or. . . ."

"You take Louis," said Sissy. "And it looks like you have a visitor." She pointed to the boy in sunglasses.

"That's just a student," said Lola. "UT's ten blocks south."

"So people park right in front of your house?" asked Sissy. That this did not happen in Midland (or nice neighborhoods, for that matter) went without saying.

Lola held the baby to her collarbone, patting him a bit roughly. "They do," she said.

"Mmm," said Sissy. "Well, let me get my bag." She lugged her own suitcase up the walkway and into the front door, which opened on a living room. It appeared that someone had taken a bag of diapers and baby toys and dumped the bag on the floor.

"I wanted to clean up . . . ," said Lola.

"No matter," said Sissy gaily. Perhaps they would give Emmett a cleaning girl for Christmas.

Lola had affixed the baby to her nipple, whoa, so Sissy busied herself looking at the bookshelves, at the weird artwork, at the sole souvenir from her eldest son's wedding day: a snapshot of the happy couple holding glasses of champagne in a cheapie Las Vegas chapel. Sissy had hired a photographer for the celebration in Midland, but the professional photographs were nowhere to be seen. Sissy and Preston's home was filled with them, ensconced in silver and cowhide frames.

The baby was blessedly quiet as he nursed, and Lola turned her sleepy gaze on Sissy. Emmett had called his mother the week before and told her he was worried about his wife. Actually, what he had said was, "How would you feel about a spring trip to Austin, Mom?" But Sissy was no dope—she could read between the lines.

"I can't believe you did this twice," said Lola.

Sissy smiled distantly. She knew Lola wanted to bond with her, and she wasn't interested. The way people talked nowadays, all about *bonding* and *disrespecting*—Sissy didn't mind watching low-class people on television talk about their problems, but she was having none of it. "Oh, well," she said now.

"Didn't you think it was hard?" Lola persisted. The poor girl had always been insecure, a fact she tried to mask with beer and bravado. Sissy didn't know who Lola was trying to impress with her exhaustive antics: river rafting, veterinary school. This girl had derailed Emmett's promising career with BP so she could learn how to spay and neuter pets. Honestly! It was a lucky thing UT had an open position in the Geology Department.

Sissy supposed it was some sort of reaction to Lola's parents' messy divorce, or maybe it was something feminist. When she thought of her daughter-in-law, Sissy hoped Lola would try to enjoy life's quiet pleasures—a simmering sauce, the hush that falls over a house when well-tended children are asleep.

"Sissy?" said Lola, her voice wavering with the threat of tears.

"Well," said Sissy, "I think I'll find my room and freshen up!" Leaving Lola anchored to the (unattractive) couch, Sissy wandered past the kitchen and into the back rooms. The nursery featured the beautiful maple crib she had sent from Graham Krackers in Midland, and another room held a futon bed piled high with dirty laundry. Sissy was adaptable—though oil had been discovered on her grandpa's ranch before she was born, she had not been spoiled, like some girls in town—so she filled her arms with laundry and called out, "Lola, where's the washing machine?"

There was a muffled response. Sissy said, "Sorry?"

"We don't have one!" Lola cried.

Well, well. It was not Sissy's place to judge. She dumped the clothes back where she had found them and shouldered her Coach purse. In the living room, Lola was holding her sleeping son and crying. "I'm so tired," she said when Sissy approached.

"Where do you keep the car keys?" asked Sissy.

"And the dishwasher is *broken*," sobbed Lola. She would come out of this, Sissy was certain. In the meantime, Sissy would employ her second-favorite motto: When in doubt,

spend. (Her favorite motto was: Raise kids in Midland, raise
hell in Dallas.) In a bowl on the kitchen counter, she found
the keys to the Ford Escape they had given Lola and Emmett
for their anniversary.

"Where are you going?" said Lola, as Sissy walked past
her, heading outside and to the car, her heels clicking on the
pavement.

At the Hancock Shopping Center, which Sissy found
after driving around for a bit, she bought a washing machine,
dryer, dishwasher, queen-size bed, and ice-cream maker. She
bought towels, sheets, a set of knives, and a few adorable
baby outfits. (Who knew Sears had baby clothes?) The appli-
ance salesman gave her the phone number of Merry Maids,
and Sissy booked an appointment for a full cleaning that
afternoon. Emmett had taken a pay cut when he left BP,
Sissy knew, but everyone deserved a washing machine.
Sissy remembered something about Lola being interested in
movies (this was before she found her calling with animals)
so Sissy bought a DVD player and plasma-screen television as
well. And a DVD of *Giant*. Then she went next door to the
H-E-B grocery store and filled a cart with groceries, beer, and
wine. What on earth had Lola's mother been doing during
her visit?

By the time Sissy returned, Lola was asleep on the couch,
Louis still as a stone on her chest. A Mexican soap opera
blared from the crummy little television. On top of the television were rabbit ears! Sissy hadn't seen those in years. She put
down her grocery bags and stepped slowly toward her grandson, just to make sure he was breathing. When she was a few

inches away, Louis opened his eyes. He took her in, gazing at Sissy, staring straight at her, unblinking.

Sissy sank to the (dirty) floor, not breaking her eye contact with the baby. Soon, Lola would wake, and her neediness and her chatter would resume. Lola wanted to *connect* to Sissy, but Sissy had made peace with only having sons long ago. Unfortunately, the saying had turned out to be true: A daughter's a daughter all your life, a son's your son till he takes a wife. Emmett called her once a month, maybe, and Preston Junior, now engaged to a hostess at Bikini's Bar and Grill, never called at all.

Sissy remembered when she was Lola's age and Preston had just moved them all to Libya in the search for more oil. After three excruciatingly sober weeks in Brega, Preston had arrived home one evening with an idea and a booklet called *The Blue Flame.* "We're going to make liquor ourselves," he said. "If I don't have a cocktail in the evening, I'm going to impale myself on Emmett's *jambiya.*" (Preston had bought his son the dagger at the old market, and it was Emmett's most prized possession.)

"I completely agree," said Sissy. "How are we going to do it?"

Preston, his long, thin nose in a book as usual, held up his palm in a distracted gesture that meant *shut up.* Sissy was just getting used to his lack of attention. Where once she had felt a flare of anger when he ignored her, now she felt a quiet resignation.

"Sorry," she said, and went to see about the boys.

By the time Sissy was thirty-two, she had two children.

Emmett, four, went to the Exxon Preschool and loved playing kickball and hanging around the pool snack bar, angling for Popsicles. He was a cunning child, constantly thinking of ways to get more sugar and attention. When Preston snapped at him—or who was Sissy kidding: when Preston yelled at him, even striking him on occasion—Emmett seemed to zone out, as if he were elsewhere. *If only,* thought Sissy. It seemed a neat trick.

Preston Junior, only one, wanted to eat sand. Sissy could not rest for a minute. There was sand outside the door of their prefab house—the streets were made of sand. What did Sissy expect, Preston had said, they were in the darn desert. He had alluded to travel in their courting, but Sissy had thought he meant a hotel room in Venice, overlooking the canal. Even the golf course in Brega was made of oiled sand and a roll of Astroturf, which you laid out and wandered along, gamely tapping your ball toward the flag. Oil and sand. And Astroturf.

Sissy played with the boys for a while, helping them stack blocks while Emmett said, "And that one's the *cave entrance* and that one's *for prisoners,*" his voice escalating in volume. The baby strutted around, his belly stuck out, shrieking.

"What's all the racket?" demanded Preston, appearing at the door of the boys' room, wearing his beleaguered expression, holding *The Blue Flame* in his hand.

"The children are playing," said Sissy.

Preston shook his head. "Okay," he said, "we need yeast and sugar. I'm going to make a still."

"Will this experiment result in a glass of chilled chardonnay?" asked Sissy.

"Fat chance," said Preston. "We're making flash, but it'll take the edge off."

Though Sissy agreed they could use a way to take the edge off, she resented his implication that their lives were so awful. Didn't he have what he wanted? He had married into an oil fortune, earned a nice engineering position, sired two healthy boys, and Sissy was a good homemaker besides. She hated the words "fat chance." They made her think of a chubby boy with glasses, crying in an elementary school gymnasium.

"How about a cool gin and tonic?" said Sissy.

"I'll do what I can," said Preston. He came closer, and surprised her by kissing her hair.

What Preston could do, it seemed, was add yeast to sugar water in a bucket, then leave the bucket to fester—or "ferment," as he called it—in their garage for a month. Then he added more water, and began to assemble a still.

*The Blue Flame* showed three different types of home stills: the Home Pot Still, the Reflux or Fractional Distillation Still, and the Sneaky Home Still, which could be stored in a dresser drawer. As Preston was an engineer by trade, and liked to make everything as difficult as possible, he chose the Fractional Distillation Still. The boys watched, rapt, as he worked with copper tubing, thermometers, glass marbles, water flow valves, and all of the stainless steel wool he'd asked a colleague to pick up during a visit stateside. He explained to Sissy that once they had the flash, they could flavor it any which way and, with a little imagination, have a full bar to offer their guests.

What guests? Sissy didn't ask. She wasn't very friendly with the other wives, it was true. Sissy liked to read murder mysteries, but motherhood had made this—her favorite pastime—nearly impossible. So she sat at the Exxon pool, trying to be happy that Emmett had friends, trying to believe that Preston Junior's shouting did not portend a loudmouth buffoon. When Emmett was invited for a play date, Sissy idled uncomfortably in the Kaysens' entrance hallway, Preston Junior on her hip, unsure whether she was supposed to stay or go. The world of expat mothers was so confusing! In Midland, she would have known what was expected of her: cookies and some juicy gossip.

After ten minutes of awkward conversation with Brigit Kaysen, no offer of drink or cookies was forthcoming, so Sissy airily alluded to a busy afternoon and left, peeking through the hedges for a last glimpse of her eldest son, who did not seem to notice her departure.

Even the baby seemed sick of her, trying to escape at the community grocery store while she placed an order for a beef fillet. ("I will call you when the beef arrives," the butcher told her. "It will be sometime in the future," he added.) When she sat down on the floor with the baby, recognizing as she had not with Emmett the limited amount of time "peekaboo" would delight a child, he wanted only to waddle away from her, into the living room, where he would upend his father's collection of Yemeni artifacts or poke his finger into an electric socket.

Preston had almost finished the still when one of his trucks broke down and he had to go to Agedabia for some parts. They had been in Brega for four months now, but Preston had not learned a word of Arabic. Well, okay, he had learned *two* words: *salaam alaykum,* which meant "hello." But repeating "hello" wasn't going to get Preston a good price on a muffler, so he needed to bring a translator. During Ramadan, Preston's translator could only travel at night, so they headed off as the sun set, unlikely cohorts on a road trip.

It was the first night Sissy had been alone since they arrived (via Europe—she had seen the inside of the Freiburg airport; apparently that was as close to glamour as she was going to get), so Sissy took out her cigarettes before Preston's taillights had disappeared from view. Her boys knew their father abhorred cigarettes—well, Emmett knew—but they would keep her little secret.

She gave them a bath, feeling tranquil as they splashed with frenetic joy and she smoked. Sometimes it was easier just not to have Preston around. He came home all worked up and grouchy and she had to appease him *and* deal with the boys. Not only did he not know how to change a diaper, he didn't even want to *hear about* dirty diapers or bottles or any bodily function. She had to be flirty and fascinated by his deadly-boring stories of plant calamities, and she had to keep the boys sweet and powder-scented. With him gone, she could let them run wild. She could join them, making goofy faces, singing songs, pretending a cottage cheese container filled with bathwater was a banana split. Or she could ignore them and read *The Murder at the Vicarage.*

In the bath, Emmett made up elaborate adventures, moving his plastic figures through the air, saying, "Aaaah! Don't worry, I'll save you!" He was lean like his father, his skin the color of uncooked chicken. The baby's dimpled bottom was pink and solid when he stood up, shouting, pounding the water with his fists.

Sissy could still feel the slow burn in her throat, still hear Preston Junior's happy sounds, though she had not had a cigarette in twenty years and Preston Junior was grown now, with a goatee and a smirk.

That night in Brega, after the boys were asleep, Sissy walked into the kitchen with a lit cigarette and rummaged in the refrigerator for soda water. When she stood, inches from the stove, she saw the Fractional Distillation Still bubbling away on the front burner. "Christ!" she yelled, throwing the cigarette into the sink and dousing it with water. A family from Houston had blown up their house the month before, trying to make booze. Sissy had seen the young daughter at the pool, her arms and legs in bandages, her skull bare where her hair had been burned off. The parents were still in the hospital, Sissy learned, and the girl was tended to by a grandmother, who fed the girl ice cream from a plastic spoon.

In the kitchen, Sissy put her hand to her chest. A slide show of horrific images played before her eyes: the explosion, ambulances, her beloved boys burned and in pain, or worse (losing either child was simply unimaginable). She took the wet cigarette and hid it in the trash can, underneath coffee grounds. Then she went and stared at Emmett and Preston, wondering how she had been so blessed.

· · ·

Baby Louis began to cry, and Lola struggled to wake. Sissy picked up her grandson, remembering to support his wobbly head. "Go back to sleep," she told Lola, who stood and shuffled toward her bedroom. But she couldn't stay quiet for long, of course, Emmett's Lola. "I'm exhausted," she said.

"Oh, sweetheart," said Sissy, almost touching Lola's sweaty hair but refraining. How could she explain the joy of that evening while Preston was away, the contentment she had felt sitting on the toilet seat, lighting one cigarette from another, oblivious? It hadn't mattered that they were in Libya. It could have been anywhere, this perfect bubble of contentment. Lola wouldn't understand that although Sissy had never passionately loved her husband, traveled to Venice, or gone river rafting, Sissy could hold the memory of that Brega evening like a secret diamond. Two naked boys in a bathtub—that, in the end, was everything.

"Will it always be so hard?" asked Lola. Louis and Lola were looking at her now, and Sissy felt an unfamiliar thrill.

"Go to sleep," said Sissy. "I'm here."

# Grandpa Fred in Love

He had met her online, my father told me. Her name was Beverly. "This time it's different," said my father. He was perspiring a bit, standing on the doorstep of my Austin, Texas, house.

"I'm happy," I said, "I'm so happy for you." Behind my father, a crew of illegal immigrants was unloading chain saws and ladders, about to go to work on my neighbor's tree. It was sick, my neighbor had told me, and so it had to go.

In his tight ROTC shirt and surf shorts, my neighbor's son, Bam, watched an immigrant scale the enormous pecan, gripping the trunk with his thighs. Bam wanted to graduate from high school and battle the insurgents. He and the immigrant were wearing the same wraparound sunglasses.

"Yeah," my father said, "it's amazing." He threw his hands open, then clasped them together. He rubbed his palms against each other like he was trying to warm them, though it was already unbearably hot and muggy. "How about a cup of joe for your old man?"

"Oh," I said, "I'm just . . . I have to take Louis off to school. I'm sorry." A bit late, my dog, Daisy, barked at my father twice, then wandered back into the living room.

"Wow," he said, "Miss Off to School." The steely meanness in his voice confirmed that he was drunk.

"Where did you find, um," I said. "Do you have a computer?"

My dad smiled condescendingly. "I have a computer," he said. He wore a Brooks Brothers suit, but it was wrinkled and smelled bad.

"Okay, great," I said. I started to close the door, muttering platitudes.

"Mom?" called Louis from the kitchen table, where he was masticating a plum. Julia, the baby, shrieked.

"I see you're in your nightgown," said my father. "Come on, let me in."

I sighed. "Lola?" called my husband, Emmett.

"I'll cut to the chase. I need a ride," said my father.

"A ride," I repeated.

"Lola?" called Emmett.

"Beverly," said my father. "She lives out in Baytown. It's our first F2F."

"Mommy," said Louis, "who's here?" He ran in from the kitchen, crashing against the couch and then my leg. There was fruit all over him. He wore Batman underpants and his Indian headdress. "Chain saw!" he screamed, pointing to the tree crew.

"It's Grandpa Fred," I said, trying to refocus his attention.

"But *why* is it Grandpa Fred?" he asked.

"Ho ho there, Chief!" cried my father. "How, Chief Louis! Are you going to put me in your cauldron and boil me up?"

Louis's eyes grew wide. "Dad," I said, "I really have to go now."

"How about lunch?" said my father. "My treat, honey."

"I'm sorry," I said.

"Honey," said my father. His eyes were bloodshot and he looked so tired.

"Lunch?" I said.

"I'll be at Ginny's Little Longhorn," said my father. "Noon?"

"Okay," I said, "okay." I shut the door.

"Mom," said Louis, "did Grandpa Fred say something about a treat?"

"No treats," I said.

Louis ran back into the kitchen, colliding with the table and then yelling, "I need a Band-Aid!"

The baby, strapped into her high chair, looked at Louis with surprise.

"Smile, baby," commanded Louis.

"She'll smile," I said.

"But *why* will she smile?" said Louis.

Emmett came into the room freshly shaven. "Your father," he announced, "is an asshole."

As promised, my father was sitting at a table at Ginny's Little Longhorn, nursing a glass of amber liquid at the crack of noon. The baby wriggled in my arms. "Oh Christ," said my father. "You can't bring a kid in here! Jesus."

My hand tightened around Julia's fat thigh. "Just tell me what you want," I said evenly.

My father sighed. "Sit down," he said. "Here, I'll take the kid." He reached out, exposing dark spots under his arms.

"I'm fine," I said.

"Remember when you were skinny?" said my father. "You had that job, at the ASPCA? Remember that?"

"That was a long time ago," I said. "Actually, I'm in veterinary school."

This was either something my father could not understand or didn't want to. He drained his drink and looked around for the waitress. "Did you hear me?" I said. "I'm going to be a doctor. A veterinarian."

"That's swell," said my father.

A woman with a great deal of blond hair approached the table. She held a spiral notebook and a pen. "Greetings," she said, looking me up and down.

"Hi," I said. "Um, I'll have some fries."

"This is a bar," said the woman.

"A saloon," my father corrected, winking.

"We don't have food," said the woman. "Unless you count

chili on Chicken Shit Bingo night. But it's not Chicken Shit Bingo night. And you don't mind my saying so, this is not a child-friendly establishment."

"I'll have a beer," I said.

My father lifted his empty glass. He shook it, and the ice clattered from side to side. I sat down.

"Where's the boy?" asked my father.

"You mean Louis?" I said. "You mean your grandson, Louis?"

"Who the fuck else would I mean?" said my father.

"He's at nursery school," I said.

"Nursery school?" said my father.

"Remember? Like Christ's Church," I said. The baby began to wail. "You used to drive me some mornings," I said, "to Christ's Church. In the convertible."

"I'll get right to it," said my father. "I'll cut to the chase." I bounced Julia, but she did not stop crying. Her face grew red.

"I can't drive," said my father. "I lost my license. . . ." He closed his eyes and waved his fingers. "Anyway," he said, "I told Beverly I'd come. I really think this is love, honey. I don't know if you can understand that."

"Dad," I said, "I'm married. I understand love."

"Right, sure," said my father, dismissing Emmett and our ten years together with a swipe of his glass. "So it's just a few hours away. I want to start this out right. I mean, I can't take a bus, you know!" His voice grew louder and louder, competing with Julia's cries.

"You could be sober," I said, standing. I slipped Julia onto my hip and swayed. Pain shot through my back, and the baby opened her mouth and screamed. She had two bottom teeth. "I have to nurse her," I said.

"For the love of Christ," said my father disgustedly. I bit my tongue. Literally, I did: I bit my tongue. "Your mother never did that with you," mused my father. "Bottles and bottles of milk."

I thought of my mother for a moment, alone in her condominium. I vowed to call her that afternoon, and I knew what she'd say when I did: "Lola! What a fabulous surprise!"

I walked out of Ginny's Little Longhorn. The hot air slapped me in the face. I got in my minivan, started the engine, and latched Julia onto my breast. She was almost a year old—not too old to nurse. Not quite a year old.

When Julia was sated, I settled her in her car seat. Her head tipped over and rested on her chins. Her mouth was slack, eyes closed. She had a bit of brown hair, and it curled away from her face. Her nose was a tiny comma, though her presence in my life seemed to be more of a period, or an endless ellipsis. My "semester off" had ended four months ago, and the thought of all the years I still had in front of me was daunting.

But I'd made it through the first day of Anatomy, when I'd met my dog cadaver, George W. I'd studied the bodies of cats, goats, even a horse. The horse cadavers were stored in a walk-in freezer, held upright by meat hooks. Each morning, we'd wheel our cadaver to the front like dry cleaning. I was happy to be studying something clear and tangible: how to set a bone, remove a tumor, even how to euthanize. When I brought Daisy to the vet, I'd sit in the waiting room and think, *Someday, I'll be the one behind that door.* I'd return to school in the fall, or perhaps the spring.

I got back in the driver's seat and fiddled with the radio. Billy Joel, NPR, some country singer, Red Hot Chili Peppers, some country singer, Mexican. Back to Billy Joel on his down eastern Alexa, cruising through Block Island Sound. In the rearview mirror, I looked strangely pretty, flushed and dewy. A young mother, a doctor-to-be. I straightened my glasses.

My father was knocking on the window of the minivan.

"I'm sorry, Dad," I said, opening the glass a few inches. "The baby has an appointment with the pediatrician this afternoon. My hands are tied."

"Hm," said my father thoughtfully. "I did wonder . . ."

"Wonder what?" I said, my voice brittle and frightened. My father held my gaze. For this, I loved him.

"I did wonder," he said softly, "about the baby."

My breath caught, and then resumed. "Get in," I said to my father. I didn't need to ask him twice.

As I drove down Burnet, I thought about the pool party. Something had happened at the pool party. It was a work event for Emmett, welcoming a new researcher to the department.

I hadn't known if there would be swimming. I had dressed Louis in a polo shirt and khaki shorts and squeezed the baby into a dress with matching bloomers. I brought bathing suits for the kids in my enormous bag, which also held diapers, swimmy diapers, wipes, fruit snacks, Operation Iraqi Freedom figurines from our neighbor Bam, mini cheese circles, assorted sticks that Louis had handed me (*Mom, this one is a sword, not a gun!*), a small sock or two, receipts, a tampon, half a bagel, and an orange. That bag—and the car, which I treated like an extension of my bag—drove Emmett wild. *I mean,* he'd say, some Saturday when he'd drunk too much coffee and paced around for too long, *something spilled in there, some juice . . . and you never even cleaned it up!* It wasn't juice, I didn't tell him. It was ice cream, from when Louis had upended a bowl of cookies and cream on my lap. I hadn't cleaned my lap, either.

"Hold my hand," said Emmett, after we parked and unstrapped the children. For a moment, I thought he was talking to me.

The Austin Country Club reminded me of the Apawamis Club in Westchester where my mother worked as the tennis pro after Dad left us, and I felt a twinge of dusty shame. I had hated hanging out at Apawamis, where I couldn't order a snack with my member number. After her lessons, my mom might get a free Fudgsicle to share with me, but it was always a favor, never an entitlement.

At the party, Emmett chatted with his colleagues. I sat by the baby pool watching Louis splash around in his Bob the Builder bathing suit. I held Julia in my lap. At some point, Emmett brought me a plate of barbecue and a plastic fork, but no napkin.

Above the big pool, there was a diving board. Kids hurled themselves into the water, crashing as cannonballs. Louis watched hungrily, and when some smaller kids jumped from the board to their parents, he begged for a turn. "Get your daddy," I told him. Emmett was listening to his boss intently, an oatmeal cookie in his hand. Conversation about the war drifted in my direction: *Stable government in the Middle East . . . Exxon chomping at the bit . . . Lord knows, you can't shock-and-awe twice.*

I knew my husband believed we had to stay the course in Iraq. He was not the type to cut and run, even if the situation sucked. And sure enough, Emmett's voice rose above the din: *At some point, though, a mistake becomes a decision, whether you like it or not.* In this, my husband and I were fundamentally different. In my opinion, a mistake required a getaway.

Louis ran at top speed from the baby pool to his father, leaping into Emmett and almost knocking him down. Emmett bent to talk to his son.

"How old is the baby?" said a heavyset woman in jeans, easing into the chair next to me.

"Her name's Julia," I said, turning her to the lady, so she could see her chubby cheeks and bright eyes. "She's eleven months. Eleven and a bit."

Her smile faltered, but she reached out a jeweled finger. Julia ignored it.

"She's . . . is she sitting up? Crawling all over?" said the woman.

"Oh, well," I said. I speared a round slice of sausage with my fork, dipped it into thick sauce. I ate the sausage and stood. The woman smiled politely, and I walked toward the diving board.

It was getting dark, and the lifeguard had climbed off his chair and was standing by the side of the pool, his red flotation device under his arm. Most kids were out of the water, lounging on the lawn in drying bathing suits.

Emmett was in the pool, his milky skin almost blue in the evening light, his sandy hair wet. He was inches from the end of the diving board, where Louis crouched nervously. I stood next to the lifeguard. "It's his first time off a diving board," I said.

"Yikes," said the lifeguard.

Emmett coached Louis to sit on the board, his legs dangling. My son extended a foot, and my husband pulled on the toes. Then he moved a few feet back.

"I should stop this," I said to the lifeguard nervously. He didn't answer, just watched intently.

Emmett said, "One, two, come on, Louis! Louis, on three!"

"You don't have to jump!" I cried, but Louis half-fell, half-jumped into the water. I grabbed the lifeguard's arm.

The woman appeared at my side. "It's none of my business," she said. "But maybe you should have the baby evaluated. I'm a neurologist. It's important to detect, um. The earlier the better . . ."

I didn't look at the woman. I looked at the pool. Emmett lunged for Louis but missed him, and he sank like a stone, his blond hair visible and then less so as he descended. Emmett dove underwater, and for a moment everything stopped. The woman was still talking. Julia rested her head on my sunwarmed shoulder. Emmett surfaced, my son sputtering in his arms.

I told my father to fasten his seat belt and I rolled the window back up and put the car in reverse. To reach Baytown, we would head south, and then east.

"I'm supposed to meet Beverly for lunch tomorrow," said my father. "We can make a day of it, get some authentic Tex-Mex. I'll find my way back, Lola, you don't even have to wait around."

"Baytown's just three hours," I said. "I'll take you there, but then I have to come home."

"Did I say Baytown?" said my father. "I meant New Orleans."

I didn't answer.

"You'd have to reschedule some things, I admit," said my father, "but it is the Big Easy, after all."

I hesitated, thinking about another day without having to see the doctor, even if it was a day in a minivan, followed by a night in some skuzzy motel, then a long drive home. In fact, I'd probably have to postpone Julia's evaluation for two days, maybe even a week. By which time, who knew? She might be smiling and holding up her head, even crawling. I put on my blinker.

I turned on Avenue F and drove to Louis's nursery school. I found my son sprawled in a beanbag, wearing My Little Pony panties. "Whoa," said my father. "What the hell is going on here?"

"His underwear was wet from the sprinkler," declared a little girl. "So I gave him my spare pair." Louis nodded seriously, verifying her account. From across the dirt field that served as Creativity Corner's playground, Louis's teacher, Roy, waved lazily, his python tattoo vivid in the bright sun.

"I'm taking Louis with me," I called, gathering the clothes in his cubby.

"Rock on," said Roy.

"Are they trying to make him into a gay or what?" my father said loudly.

Back in the minivan, I explained to Louis that we were headed on a road trip to New Orleans. I called Emmett's office, but when I got his voice mail, I hung up. "*Why* are we headed on a road trip to New Orleans?" asked Louis.

"We're going to find a pretty lady named Beverly," said my father.

"But *why* are we going to find a pretty lady named Beverly?"

"For love, kid," said my father. "Now shut the hell up."

"Please don't tell Louis to shut the hell up," I said.

"Fair enough," said my father.

We drove in silence for about three minutes before Louis screamed, "OLD MAC DONALD'S! OLD MAC DONALD'S!"

"I could use a Quarter Pounder with Cheese," my father said. I got in the right-hand lane.

While Louis and my father went inside, I nursed the baby with the air-conditioning on. Julia ate greedily, and I stared at her beautiful face. When she was finished, I propped her in the passenger seat, but she slumped over. I propped her again, and cheerfully, she slumped again. I took her in my arms, and contemplated my life. If only she would stay small, I thought. I wouldn't mind having a baby forever if she were small. It was the adult baby I was scared of, lying around the living room in pajamas, watching *Pimp My Ride*.

The door to the minivan slid open. "Grandpa Fred," Louis was saying, "did the gook die, when you shot him in the head?"

My father had the dignity to look at me sheepishly.

"Of course not," I said soothingly.

"He went to the hospital," said my father. "Where all is magically fixed." This barb was in reference to the last time I had seen my father, a year before, when Emmett and I had presented him with a one-way ticket to the Promises rehab facility. Presumably, he had not found all the answers there.

I drove for a while on 290, and the city ended. There was a stretch of farmland before the Houston sprawl began. There was the road to Dime Box, Texas, where Emmett and I had picked out a puppy, back when I got accepted to vet school and we thought a puppy would teach us all we needed to know about caring for small things. But the puppy didn't interrupt us when we tried to talk, and the puppy didn't exhaust us past wanting to care for each other. The puppy didn't require ten phone calls and fifty bucks for me to have a pizza and a pitcher of beer with my husband. We didn't wonder, while making love, if the puppy would hear us.

"Dime Box!" I called out gaily as we passed, thinking of Emmett in the canvas sneakers he'd lost years ago (and that Ouray Volunteer Fire Department T-shirt, now in tatters), petting golden retrievers and deciding which one to fall for. Because she had jumped into Emmett's lap, we had chosen Daisy, the last girl left from the previous litter. She moved awkwardly on her big paws. All the way home, we had laughed as she climbed over us, almost causing us to have an accident when she scrambled down by the brake and Emmett practically stepped on her, trying to slow the car.

"Why did you say *Dime Box,* Mommy?"

I opened my mouth, but it seemed impossible to explain all that Dime Box had meant to me, to us. I peeked at Julia via my Baby in Sight Back Seat Mirror. She stared brightly ahead. She didn't smile, which was another sign. "It's just the name of a town," I said.

"But *why* is it the name of a town?" said Louis.

"Sometimes," said my father, "things just are what they are, bud."

Louis considered this for about five seconds.

"But—"

"No more talking!" said my father harshly. "Grandpa Fred needs a nap, and all this racket is giving me a headache."

The baby began to cry, crammed into her infant seat, and my father yelled, "Shut up!"

In the distance, I saw a sign for the Brenham bus depot, a beacon. I followed the arrow, then pulled the car off the road. Julia continued her crying, and Louis began to whimper. "For the love of GOD," said my father, "I'd rather take the Bonanza bus!"

The bus station's front window framed an old couple holding hands. They gazed at us placidly. If I turned around,

I knew, I would make it back to Austin in time to see the pediatrician. I had read about autism online, and I was deeply afraid that something was wrong.

But unlike my father, who had headed to work one morning and never returned, Emmett would take in all the doctor had to tell us, and then he would make something from *The Thrill of the Grill* for dinner. We would put our children to bed, and sit on the porch swing. Maybe we would cry, and then we would hold each other. When Julia woke us, Emmett would stumble from sleep and pick her up, and then he would scramble eggs. It was worth saying that though my genes were half my father's, I would be there too, finding Louis's Operation Iraqi Freedom figurines, using leaves and twigs to make them a house.

"Get out," I told my father.

"Oh really?" he said.

"You heard me," I said.

"You are some piece of work," said my father. "Kicking a man when he's down." I didn't say anything, just opened my bag and found my wallet amidst the diapers and snacks. I handed my father a twenty. He looked incredulous, his mouth open and his cunning brain firing. "Well, good luck with the retard," he said, probably thinking I would answer, and the conversation would continue. But I reached across him and opened his door.

"Say good-bye to Grandpa Fred!" I said cheerily.

Louis stopped sniffling. "Bye, Grandpa Fred," he said. The baby blinked, and I imagined a hint of a grin, but then she started crying again. My father shook his head as if I had disappointed him but he had expected it, pocketed the twenty, and got out. I drove away, leaving my father walking purposefully toward the Brenham depot.

"Dime Box!" I called, as we passed the turnoff on the way home. Gaily, Louis called out, "Dime Box!" Maybe even the baby would say *Dime Box* someday.

I didn't hear from my father for two years. The day he called, Emmett was planting the purple passion vine he'd bought me for my thirty-eighth birthday. He had come home from work with the flowering plant, and I'd met him at the front door with a big kiss and a packed suitcase. My mother, Nan, had flown in to watch the kids, and I had splurged, renting a cabin on the Llano River. For four days, Emmett fished and drank beer, and I sat by the river, paging through my old Anatomy textbook. We ate pork chops and pickles at Cooper's Barbecue. One afternoon, Emmett had two strikes and one catch, though he threw the fish back. He walked toward me in his wet waders and boots, three days unshaven. "I am so damn happy," he said, when he reached me.

The day my father called, Louis, in a baseball cap, was standing next to Emmett, holding a shovel that was too big for him. Julia was organizing her plastic animals on the kitchen floor. Sweet old Daisy was asleep, as usual, inside a slice of light. Watching my family, I was filled with a quiet peace.

Our next-door neighbor, whose son, Bam, was being buried at the Veterans Cemetery that afternoon, was lying on his lawn, staring at the space where his tree had been. He wore Bam's sunglasses against the blinding rays. In Iraq, my neighbor had told me, Bam had thrown himself atop a grenade, saving six other men.

On my answering machine, my father said that he had ended up back out west. It was different this time, he said. He'd finally found it—real romance, the real deal—with a woman in Montana, the Last Best Place.

# Acknowledgments

Thank you, Gina Centrello, for believing in my short stories. I am grateful to Brian McLendon for the husband's point of view, and to Kim Hovey for her enthusiasm and friendship. Thanks to Clay Smith for publishing my first short story, and to M.M.M. Hayes, Jeff Boison, Whitney Pastorek, Andy Spear, Rob Spillman, and Michael Ray for supporting my work. ASG, thank you for encouraging me from the start, when we waited by our Missoula mailboxes for rejection slips. I found a home in Austin thanks to my friends Juli Berwald, Lacey Schmelzle, Caroline Wilson, Ingrid Johansen, Terry Benaryeh, Emily Hovland, Laurie Duncan, Erin Kinard, Becca Cody, Paula Disbrowe, Mary Maltbie,

Jaye Joseph, and Will Heron. This collection would not exist without my editor, Anika Streitfeld, who cares deeply about words, makes my writing life a joy, and believes *beautiful* should replace *lonely*. Thanks to my agent, Michelle Tessler, for her hard work and thoughtful insights. (Also, thank you to Jack, for reminding me that leaves and twigs can make a house.) For Napa weekends, wise advice, and happy phone calls, thank you to Mary-Anne Westley (the most gorgeous grandmother in Savannah), Liza Bennigson (who lights up the room), and Sarah McKay (who somehow manages to mix glamour and brilliance with motherhood). WAM and THM, I love you a million stars. Tip, thank you for inspiring all my love stories, and for filling my life with grace.

$\mathcal{L}$ove Stories
IN THIS TOWN

Amanda Eyre Ward

A READER'S GUIDE

# A Conversation with
# Amanda Eyre Ward

**Random House Reader's Circle: Most of your readers know you as a novelist, but you have actually been a short-story writer for longer than you have been a novelist. Can you talk a little about how and when you first started writing stories?**

**A:** I went to Williams College, where I signed up for Jim Shepard's Introductory Fiction Workshop. I showed up the first day to find the room packed. Jim (Professor Shepard to me then) told us we could submit one story, and he would choose the members of the small class and post a list on his office door. Many of the other students had folders of stories, neatly stapled, but although I was an avid reader, I had never

written a story before. I was reading Denis Johnson and Raymond Carver at that time. I typed all night on my Brother
word processor, creating a story about a speed-addled trucker
on an all-night run. I think the trucker ended up in a "wall of
flames." I wasn't hopeful, so I didn't even check the list on
Jim's door. When a friend congratulated me, I had already
missed the first class. I showed up the next week, and Jim
said, "Now where were you for the first meeting, Amanda?"

"I was at the mall buying sneakers."

"At the mall buying sneakers," Jim said. "Class," he said,
"this is what we call *off to a flying start.*"

After this "flying start," I never looked back. Jim taught
us what a short story was. He also showed his students, by
example, that one could write fiction, that it was possible to
study and work hard and become an author, the same way
others might become a banker or a hockey coach. This was a
revelation to me. My father remembers a moment in his car
when I opened the envelope with my final grade in Jim's
class—a B-minus—and burst into tears. It was the only
grade I cared about, and by the end of college, writing a
beautiful short story was the only thing I wanted to do. I
wanted to be Raymond Carver, Rick Bass, and Richard
Ford, so after a year abroad, I moved to Montana.

**RHRC: How do you think your writing has changed since
then?**

**A:** In Missoula, I was imitating writers I loved. My professor
at the University of Montana, William Kittredge, taught me

to expand my repertoire, to rely on honesty—on my story, what I had to say—instead of shock value. I expanded my reading list, devouring Paul Bowles, Mona Simpson, James Salter, Katherine Anne Porter, Michael Cunningham, and Jennifer Egan. I began to slow my sentences down, working to trust character development, to choose sincerity over sarcasm. He also told me that if I wanted to be a novelist, I needed to move to where my best friend was and write my damn book.

**RHRC: One of the stories in this collection grew out of a story you wrote as a graduate student. Can you tell us about that?**

**A:** "Miss Montana's Wedding Day" was my first published short story. It won third prize in the *Austin Chronicle* Short Story Contest, and when they called to tell me, I was busy at my latest job, answering phones at a software company. I told my colleagues the exciting news, and one called out, "Hey everyone! Amanda's going to have one of her stories published in the *Pennysaver*!"

It was strange to revisit the story. I was a heartbroken graduate student when I wrote it, so it was interesting to peek back in time, to see how I viewed love. I now understand some things about the character Lola that I didn't understand then. Sometimes that happens—I don't know *why* a story or book isn't working, and I give up, but when I revisit the work later, some event or knowledge enables me to understand the piece.

On a technical level, I liked to rely on pointing out local

color a bit too much, I think. I wanted the setting to tell the reader things that could be conveyed only by allowing readers into Lola's thoughts. (I was trying to be like Paul Bowles . . . his use of setting is unsettling and amazing.) My editor, Anika Streitfeld, has worked on all four books of mine, and she's really encouraged me to let readers into a character's thoughts. Almost every first draft comes back with pages of Anika's red-penned notes saying, "What is she thinking here?" and "A bit about what he's feeling."

The end of "Miss Montana's Wedding Day," when Abe says, "There are no love stories in this town," seemed very bleak and revelatory to me when I wrote the story. Instead of a sad statement about Lola's future, I now see it as a harbinger of things to come: Lola will leave that town, and she will have a love story of her own.

**RHRC: What do you usually start with when you're setting out to write a short story? How do you know that the material is better suited to a story than to a novel?**

**A:** Generally, I think in "scenes." I'll see an image—a woman sitting at an airport bar, or a man in a canoe. So for "The Stars Are Bright in Texas," for example, I saw a couple house hunting, an unhappy woman in the back of a minivan. I'm interested in places like The Woodlands, outside Houston, so I set the story there. As Kimberly and Greg moved through their house hunt, however, I wasn't sure if the "scene" would be a story, a piece of a novel . . . I didn't know. And when it ended, with Kimberly walking toward Greg at the airport, I just knew the story was over. I didn't need to follow them back to Bloomington, or see how they ended up. I realized that the story was an exploration of loss counterbalanced with hope. And whether or not that hope was fulfilled wasn't what I wanted to write about.

On the other hand, I am now working on a novel, and as I'm following the characters through the scenes, I just keep thinking more of their past and future, and how their stories will dovetail. I don't know how to explain it—I know there's a novel (or maybe ten) there. I wish I knew how it would all work out, but as long as the images keep coming, I feel lucky.

**RHRC: "Should I Be Scared" and "The Way the Sky Changed" take place in the wake of 9/11. Did you write them soon after the events in the story occurred? Were these difficult stories to write?**

**A:** I am from Rye, New York, a town that was deeply affected by 9/11. There are so many heartbreaking stories from my town—families who lost fathers, families who lost sons. And I hadn't lived in Rye for a long time, so it always seemed somewhat idyllic in my memory, a childhood place full of walks to school with my best friend, white picket fences, and lemonade stands. After the collapse of the towers, I was devastated—it seemed impossible that not even Rye was safe.

I remember I went to a reading that week, it was Jonathan Franzen reading from *The Corrections* at Book People in Austin. I raised my hand and asked him if he'd ever be able to write about normal, calm life again. He thought my question was strange, and said, "Of course I will." (Everyone reacted in a different way—in several interviews since, I've read Franzen's take on the 9/11 aftermath, and how it has, in some ways, affected his work.) I drove home that night wondering if I was crazy for feeling so frightened. I wrote "Should I Be Scared?" soon after 9/11, and I have to admit that I did, indeed, get a prescription for ciprofloxacin. I hid the pills in a baggie in my utensil drawer.

I didn't write "The Way the Sky Changed" for a while. I actually wrote a short play first about a policeman coming to a 9/11 widow's apartment with her husband's remains. As time passed, the aftermath of 9/11 became so awful it was surreal—the hairbrushes, the bones. I know that many people have been hurt around the world by acts of terrorism, but I don't think I'll ever get over September 11.

**RHRC: "Shakespeare.com" also captures a particular time and place—the Internet boom in San Francisco. Can you tell us about the evolution of this story?**

**A:** I worked at many different jobs during the Internet boom—I was just out of graduate school, and though newspapers were calling the time a boom, I had never known anything different. At one point, I got a job as a "Curriculum Developer" for a company in Austin. We had a great time, and most of the details about margarita machines and puppies are true. But there was always a gnawing sense that we might not all strike it rich with this venture.

I guess I like the idea that Mimi is knocking at the door of the real world—parenthood, responsibility—but not quite walking through it yet.

The first draft of the story ended with Mimi realizing that she is not pregnant, and the company getting more money and Girl Scout cookies. I sent the story out and was contacted by M.M.M. Hayes, the editor of *Story Quarterly.* We had a great conversation about the story, and she said that she felt I had dropped the ball at the end. She told me she wanted stories that "opened out," or gave a reader some wider sense of the world.

I took her comments to heart, and I'm really proud of the final story. Like the dinosaurs, Mimi and Leo are about to get hit: by parenthood, by adulthood, by world events like 9/11.

**RHRC: As the title suggests, place plays an important role in this collection. How did you come up with the settings for the various stories? How is writing about places you have lived in different from writing about places you haven't?**

**A:** Luckily, in my search for a home, I've lived in many places. And place is very important to me. I can hardly write about a place I don't really know, though it's often years after I leave a place that I want to write about it. Some time needs to pass before I can figure out what a place has meant to me, what I've learned there. But for the stories to work together, they couldn't all be set in the same towns. "Shakespeare .com," for example, was moved from Austin to San Francisco. My editor's husband, Jared Luskin, had worked in an Internet start-up, so he was able to help me relocate the story without too much trouble. I kept some of the Austin bars, however. Jovita's is here in Austin—you won't find it south of Market.

In general, I don't like to write about places I don't know well. There's no substitute for walking the streets of a city, sitting at a local diner, driving the same streets every day to get to work.

Now that I've settled in Austin, Texas, for a while if not forever, I'm interested in neighbors, in the way proximity leads to friendship and dependence. I'm also able, once in a while, to turn off the fiction writer's radar, to not always be noting the local customs, as if I'm in a foreign country and not in my yard. But that's another story.

**RHRC: Can you talk about how Lola developed?**

**A:** Well, originally, she was named Vera, for one thing. When I realized I had enough stories for a collection, I wasn't sure which stories were about the same character. Many of the women were the same age, and many were married (as I am) to a geologist.

It took some time to trust myself and figure out which characters were connected and how ... putting all the stories together was very difficult. Each story was written to be its own world, to stand alone. I had to think about how the book would flow thematically. I feel as if I have a sense about how to structure a novel at this point, but putting this collection together was challenging. I am still changing the order of the stories—even as the book is about to be typeset.

**RHRC: Do you think you will continue to write about Lola?**

**A:** I'm sure I will. I love her, and I can't wait to see how her life turns out. I hope she goes back to vet school. I had also written a scene in which she and Emmett are much older and get matching tattoos—I'd like to use that scene someday.

**RHRC: Some of these stories went through a number of rounds of editing. How does that process work? How do you know when a story is finished?**

**A:** I always feel scared to say that a story is finished, I think. Honestly, I could keep working on all of these stories. But at some point, you do feel that a subtle balance has been achieved—the characters' actions feel true. But Anika and I worked on some of these stories through a dozen or more drafts. I would generally send her a story, and she would send detailed notes, or give me a call. Then I'd let her comments sit with me, and go back at the story. I always get very upset at this stage—hacking away at a story's foundations makes me feel that the whole thing will come crashing down. But Anika has edited all three of my novels, so I take solace when she tells me, "You were just as nervous with *How to Be Lost*." Each time, it feels like a new terror. Anyway, sometimes a day, sometimes a week, later I would send

Anika a new draft. One thing I've learned through editing these stories is that sometimes Anika will say, "This ending isn't working," but I don't have to fix the ending. I have to fix, perhaps, the character's morning, or her job, or her husband . . . the scenes leading up to the last scene. Sometimes the problem is where I least expect it. Anika might feel that the character's actions are not working, but sometimes it may not be the actions but the way I set them up. And there's never a simple answer. For example, in one draft of "Motherhood and Terrorism," the husband was named Anthony, and he was an investment banker. We went through numerous drafts before I realized that the female character was, in fact, Lola, and the husband was Emmett. So Anthony got sent to the graveyard. There's a big pile of discarded characters for this book. I think of them all in a serene graveyard, waiting to be exhumed.

**RHRC: What was it like to have your first book in the world, to become a published author?**

**A:** When my first novel, *Sleep Toward Heaven,* was published, I had listened to a hundred readings, and had always thought about what it might feel like to be the one behind the podium . . . I never thought I'd be wearing a maternity dress. The publication process was different from what I had expected, actually. I had thought so much about what the cover would look like, what it would be like to see the book on the shelf, but some steps surprised me. I had long phone calls with my agent, Michelle Tessler, and Anika—after having the characters live in my imagination for so long, it was an honor to have thoughtful talks about them, to have Anika and Michelle's perspective on who they were, and how they developed. I didn't realize how much I'd enjoy that. And then seeing my words typeset—that was really exciting. But even as I loved having my book in the world and giving readings, I ached to get back to writing. I can dress up and speak to a crowd—I love it, in fact—but I am most comfortable alone in my bathrobe, reading or writing. It's really strange to answer questions about the solitary process of writing. I don't really know how it all works—I'm still learning—and I feel I might jinx something.

**RHRC: You mentioned Bill Kittredge's advice to "Move to where your best friend is and write your damn book." What advice do you give to aspiring writers? Is there anything you wish you had known, or done differently?**

**A:** I think you have to love the writing, and have faith that someday there will be an agent and an editor who get what you're trying to do, and who want to work with you. But it always comes back to the blank page, to a new morning in front of the computer screen. After a series of jobs that were somewhat related to publishing, I finally started working at jobs that didn't use the same part of my brain as my writing. I knew it might take years to get published (and it did take years . . . ten years), so I wanted to enjoy myself in the meantime. I set up an office in my house, splurged on beautiful journals and a big bulletin board for mapping out story lines and tacking up stories from the *New York Times* that captured my interest. I tell students to take themselves, and their writing, seriously. I also read for hours every day. After years of trying to write for my professors or for my fellow students, I now aim to write a book that I want to read.

**RHRC: How does your reading life affect your writing life?**

**A:** The other morning I woke up at about three a.m. I lay awake in the dark and wondered what the point of all my reading was. In the time I've spent lying around with books, I could have become a pediatrician—or a rocket scientist. And it's not that I like to talk about what I've read: For the most part, my reading is completely selfish. I leave books half unread, and I was kicked out of my book club for never getting around to that month's pick. I don't keep up my virtual bookshelf, and I lost the little leather notebook that I bought to jot down what I'd read.

It's solitary, it's compulsive, it's expensive, and I tend to read a short story or novel and imagine that the fictional problems are my own, living half in Andre Dubus's character's sadness and half in my own life. But I can't stop. There are times that I think my reading and writing life are truer than my real life, the one I have to brush my teeth for.

Sometimes it's hard to look closely at the fragile beauty that surrounds me. I'm scared that looking too closely will mess everything up. So I read, to re-wire my brain, to expand my sense of what is possible. So that morning, at three a.m., I picked up a short-story collection and began to read. I was hoping to find solace, to find inspiration, to find my way back to sleep.

**RHRC: How do you think writing—and reading—short stories is different from writing or reading a novel?**

**A:** I guess if novels are like a long car ride, one in which you might see many glorious sights but might also run out of gas and be stuck in some strange town, short stories are like one perfect evening. There doesn't have to be a moment wasted: The moon is out, the wine is chilling, and the steaks are on the grill. A story can do anything—a gunshot can pop, a memory from long ago can alter a kiss, a cow can have a point of view. Of course, any of these events can occur in a novel, but they happen with baggage. If your main character gets shot, you have to write her through her ambulance ride and convalescence. Writing a short story, I feel freer. As a reader, a story's joys are manifold. I can read one before bed and still have time to mull it over before morning. When I begin reading a story, I never know if it will contain a lifetime (as many of Alice Munro's and Jhumpa Lahiri's stories do) or one defining moment.

I think there is a kind of magic in the books that come to a reader. A few years ago, when I was experimenting with what a short story could do, I happened to open the *New Yorker* and find "A Primer for the Punctuation of Heart Disease" by Jonathan Safran Foer. When I was learning to be sincere, I was humbled by Lorrie Moore's "People Like That Are the Only People Here: Canonical Babbling in Peed

Onk" and Jhumpa Lahiri's "A Temporary Matter." Helen Simpson inspired me to write about parenthood. And last week, a friend handed me Ben Fountain's *Brief Encounters with Che Guevara,* which is, in a word, stunning, and has inspired me to try to write about my time in Africa.

**RHRC: What are you working on now?**

**A:** I'm working on a new novel. I'm still getting to know all the characters. There are two sisters with secrets from each other, there's a new mother drinking whiskey with an elderly woman. There's a murder, and a neighborhood trying to make sense of tragedy. I've been inspired by the recent work of Francine Prose, Ann Patchett, Jonathan Franzen, Roxanna Robinson, Wally Lamb, Stewart O'Nan, and Kate Atkinson.

**Q: Would you share some of your favorite short story collections with us?**

**A:** I would love to. Here are some of my favorites, in the order that I happened to read them.

> *The Short Stories of F. Scott Fitzgerald* (I especially love "The Ice Palace.")
> *The Watch* by Rick Bass
> *Where I'm Calling From* by Raymond Carver
> *The Collected Stories of Grace Paley*

*The Collected Stories of Amy Hempel* (I never stop thinking about the friendship in "The Cemetery Where Al Jolson Is Buried.")

*Rock Springs* by Richard Ford

*Our Story Begins* by Tobias Wolff (My favorite stories are "Say Yes" and "Deep Kiss.")

*Mary and O'Neill* by Justin Cronin

*Selected Stories* by Nadine Gordimer

*A Distant Episode: The Selected Stories* by Paul Bowles

*CivilWarLand in Bad Decline* by George Saunders (especially "Offloading for Mrs. Schwartz")

*Interesting Women* by Andrea Lee (especially "The Birthday Present")

*Dusk and Other Stories* by James Salter

*Emerald City* by Jennifer Egan

*Interpreter of Maladies* by Jhumpa Lahiri

*A Stranger in this World* by Kevin Canty

*Birds of America* by Lorrie Moore

*Drown* by Junot Díaz

*Jesus' Son* by Denis Johnson

*How It Was for Me* by Andrew Sean Greer (also "The Islanders," which was published in the *New Yorker* and is so lovely I have to reread it every few months)

*Remote Feed* by David Gilbert

*Sam the Cat and Other Stories* by Matthew Klam

*Carried Away: A Selection of Stories* by Alice Munro (and later, "Deep Holes")

*We Don't Live Here Anymore* by Andre Dubus (I can't

stop thinking about "Finding a Girl in America," the last novella.)

*The Bridegroom* by Ha Jin (especially "After Cowboy Chicken Came to Town")

*The Collected Stories of Richard Yates* (especially "Oh Joseph, I'm So Tired")

*Among the Missing* by Dan Chaon

*Lucky Girls* by Nell Freudenberger

*A Relative Stranger* by Charles Baxter

*Getting a Life* by Helen Simpson

*Female Trouble* by Antonya Nelson (and later, "Shauntrelle," published in the *New Yorker*)

*Say You're One of Them* by Uwem Akpan

*Brief Encounters with Che Guevara* by Ben Fountain (especially "Rêve Haïtien")

# Reading Group Questions and Topics for Discussion

1. Though the book's title may seem romantic, it actually comes from a moment of extreme cynicism—a bartender telling Lola after her ex-boyfriend's wedding that "There are no love stories in this town." Why do you think Ward chose this as the title for the collection? Did reading these stories make you see love stories in a different light?

2. If you have read Ward's novels, did you find the tone or perspective of any of these stories familiar? How would you describe Ward's writing style? Her characters?

3. Fertility and pregnancy play a big role in a number of these stories. How do the women in these stories approach motherhood? Is it different from how their husbands seem to be approaching fatherhood? Do you see these issues representing larger themes about identity, change, or relationships?

4. The realities of living in a post-9/11 world come up in several stories—in the narrator's obsession with Cipro in "Should I Be Scared," in Lola's anxiety about living in Saudi Arabia in "Motherhood and Terrorism," and in Casey's grief in "The Way the Sky Changed." How much are these stories about a specific moment in history, and how much do they speak to broader emotional issues?

5. Ward's stories take place in a variety of "towns"— in Texas, New York, Maine, Montana—and in San Francisco. How important is setting to the stories? What do you think they mean, in particular, to Lola, who lives in a number of quite different places?

6. Like Lola and Emmett, the narrator of "Should I Be Scared?" and her husband have different interests—his in science, hers in the humanities. How does the clash between science and imagination factor into each story? How do you think it shapes each of their relationships?

7. Lola Wilkerson is at the center of six of the collection's twelve stories. Why do you think Ward devotes so much

of her collection to this character? What similarities do you see between the Lola stories and the preceding stories? What is different about these stories?

8. How do you think Lola's relationship with her father impacts her relationship with Iain, and later with Emmett?

9. Nan and Sissy are very different characters—and mothers. How do you see their personalities and parenting styles affecting their children? Do you think Lola is more similar to Nan, or is she influenced by both of them?

10. From the ceramic consultant in "Should I Be Scared?" to Kimberly's fashion design, from the Internet start-up in "Shakespeare.com" to Lola's dramatic career shift, work is a feature of many of these stories. How would you describe the role work plays in the female characters' lives? Is it different for the men?

11. From snappy comebacks to a strong sense of the absurd, humor appears in many of Ward's stories. How would you describe the way humor fits into her sensibility as a writer? What were some of your favorite funny lines or moments?

12. Do you have a favorite story in the collection? Which story did you find the saddest? The most surprising?

PHOTO: © MARY HELEN SPECHT

Amanda Eyre Ward is a graduate of Williams College and the University of Montana. She is the author of the novels *Sleep Toward Heaven, How to Be Lost,* and *Forgive Me*. Amanda's short fiction has been published in *Tin House, Zoetrope, Story Quarterly,* and the *New Delta Review*. Amanda lives with her family in Austin, Texas.

## ABOUT THE TYPE

This book was set in Granjon, a modern recutting of a typeface produced under the direction of George W. Jones, who based Granjon's design upon the letterforms of Claude Garamond (1480–1561). The name was given to the typeface as a tribute to the typographic designer Robert Granjon.